MALCOLM HAVARD career that has taken] construction, academia, tc had a love of history and

His writing career start

of successful books, he thought he'd give fiction a try, asking himself 'How hard could it be?' Fifteen years later he now suspects the answer is 'Very, very hard'. He lives in Cheshire with his partner Nicola and a grumpy cat.

Follow Malcolm on Twitter: @MalHavardWriter

THE
HONEY TALKER

MALCOLM HAVARD

Northodox Press Ltd
Maiden Greve, Malton,
North Yorkshire, YO17 7BE

This edition 2022

1

First published in Great Britain by
Northodox Press Ltd 2022

ISBN: 9781915179111

This book is set in Caslon Pro Std

Thanks to Nic and the Renegades
for putting me and Aidan on the right track.

Chapter One

It was time to leave. It was all getting too hazy, all conversation now just a buzz dulled by alcohol, the noise and the song, that song repeated for the umpteenth time. It was always in the background.

Richard lifted his pint. 'Well, that's that then, goodbye to the grey man and the bunch of back-stabbers.' He drained his glass. 'Another?'

Aidan shook his head. 'Not this time.' He stood up. 'I have to get to bed. We're going to be busy in the morning.'

Richard shrugged; his eyes on a loud, large group of women on the other side of the bar. 'Lightweight,' he said. 'The night's still young.'

Aidan followed his gaze. 'I'd only cramp your style. See you tomorrow, Rich.'

He was up and away before Richard could protest. Richard might have fifteen or more years on Aidan but his capacity for alcohol and women were legendary, so he'd learned to his cost not to try to keep pace.

'Things can only get better…'

The strains of the song that had been on repeat all night faded away as he left the bar.

Aidan laughed to himself. Yes, of course they could. They couldn't get much bloody worse.

1

But still, jaded as he was, this did feel like a new start, a change, the sweeping away of the old inertia, corruption, sleaze, of the lack of progress or ideas.

Maybe it would rub off on him.

A branch of Curry's had all the TV's on in the window. All said the same thing: Exit Poll predicts New Labour landslide. Blair's picture everywhere, grinning, waving.

Everyone was happy. People were laughing, partying. Let Richard do the same.

He knew what the election result meant for him; a lot of work. He'd be told to get quotes from the business world on how the local property industry was going to cope with Blair and Brown.

He reached his car. He only intended to get his coat out of it but now he was here and it was tempting to just get in and drive home. He shouldn't, not with what he'd put away this evening, but he was expected to be in work first thing. If he took the tram and bus, it could take an hour. In the car, it would be fifteen minutes, tops.

Sod it, he thought. He'd just drive carefully. He was sure the police would be too busy with other stuff tonight anyway.

He got in and made the usual prayer as he turned the key: please start. He'd bought the Spyder on a whim, seen it on a car lot in Salford, had been seduced by its curves and bright red paintwork but the polish had concealed a myriad of problems that had plagued him from day one. Tonight, though it started at the first pull. He smiled; maybe things were really getting better.

He pulled out without checking the mirror.

There was a blaze of lights, a car's horn was held down. Shit, whoever it was had really been moving.

'Stupid fuck, you shouldn't have been racing, should you?'

He wound down the window and gave the driver a middle finger, then put his foot down.

Time to get away. The Alfa was beautifully nimble in the city and by the time he'd reached the next straight street, a classic double row of Manchester terraces with cars parked on either side, there was no sign of the other car.

His relief was only momentary.

Brilliant blue-white headlamps appeared behind him, on full beam, then flashed as the car rushed up right behind him, the driver seemingly unaffected by the limited space caused by the unbroken line of cars lining each side of the street.

'What's wrong with you?' Aidan shouted into his mirror. 'Just fuck off.'

The sweat was pouring off him, the car's interior was bathed in light; it was as if the headlights were giving off heat like a pair of mini suns. Even with dipping his mirror, the light penetrated his retinas, cutting though them like razorblades. He could hardly see to drive.

There was a bang; one of his mirrors had gone, smashed against a parked car. Then there was another as his pursuer hit his rear bumper. It had to be something big and hefty chasing him, the impact briefly lifted the rear of the Alfa up, the engine racing as the wheels were robbed of the torque of the road surface.

'You bloody nutter!' Aidan fought to get the Alfa back under control when it landed.

That had done some damage, he was sure, but he wasn't going to stop to check. He was soon going to have bigger problems; here the other car couldn't get by but at the end of the street was a main road, wider with room to overtake.

He should stop now and face them down.

He shook his head.

No way. He didn't want a beating.

He would take his chance; maybe the police would see them, stop them. Sod the breathalyser, he'd take that now.

He turned right, towards the Quays. The other car followed and immediately tried to get by. Aidan was ready; he swung right to block him. He received a blare of the horn for his cheek and felt a slight nudge as the car hit his rear bumper again, at an angle this time. Momentarily, Aidan thought he was going to spin but he caught the slide and floored the throttle. The speed rose rapidly, 40, 50, 60...

This couldn't last, Aidan knew that, he could hear the gruff roar of the other car's engine over the scream of the Alfa; its power was obvious. It would get by.

There was a slight bend in the road. Aidan registered lights coming towards him. Small, quite dim, candles compared with the brilliant monsters that rent the darkness behind him. A small car. Close. He heard the almost timid parp of a horn. He pulled the Alfa to the left, out of the way of the oncoming car.

The next brief moments were a jumble of confused images but remained oddly clear.

The small car framed in the brilliant headlights.

A small Fiat.

Two people in it, a bearded young man and a girl, their eyes wide open in terror.

The nose of the car - for the first time Aidan recognised the make; a Bentley - appearing next to him, overtaking.

The driver looking across.

The impact with the Fiat.

The crash of metal against metal.

A dull, heavy, ominously violent thump. Breaking glass.

Then it was all snatched behind him as Aidan sped on and away.

Chapter Two

Aidan was stunned, unable to do anything other than keep driving.

The sudden darkness after the harshness of the headlights was like being plunged into icy water. He was going to be sick, yet drove on as if on automatic pilot.

The traffic lights onto the main road were on green. He turned right, though the direction didn't matter; he just needed somewhere to stop. He was shaking so much he could barely hold the steering wheel. If he continued, he was sure to either have an accident or be stopped as a drunk driver – which, of course, was exactly what he was.

There was an office building to his left, the entrance to the car park a few yards further on. Aidan signalled even though there were no other cars around and turned into it. In the car park he turned away from the building and found a space in the farthest, darkest corner and turned the engine off then sat quietly for a full two minutes before opening the door and threw up onto the tarmac.

He got out and squatted on his haunches, shaking like he had the flu. He wasn't sure how long he stayed there, a few minutes at most. He got back inside, realising that he would likely attract attention the longer he stayed. In the car's glovebox, he found a packet of tissues and cleaned up his face as best as he could, then sat in the driver's seat and stared straight ahead.

What should he do?

He'd left the scene of an accident, an offence in its own right.

He should go back - but what if he'd been seen? The police

would breathalyse him; he'd be well over the limit. The car was also missing a wing mirror and its MOT had expired at least two months ago. He'd meant to sort it out, book it in but hadn't got around to it. It was a 'do it tomorrow' job.

As usual with Aidan, tomorrow had never come.

The police would be there. He'd be in pretty deep trouble if he went back. There were at least three strikes against him.

They'd throw the book at him. He'd lose his licence. Lose his job.

Yet he had to go back. Common humanity required him to go. There could be people injured – in fact at the speeds involved there had to be – it was shameful not to, he was a witness.

More than a witness, he was involved.

There was one more thing. He was a reporter, yeah a pretty crap one, just a business correspondent but a reporter nonetheless. He should report and investigate. It was his job.

What a fool he was! That gave him a legitimate reason for being at the crash. He'd be there to do his job.

Maybe that would cover him.

In the distance, he heard a siren; that was it. Help was on the way. They'd be all right.

However, there was still the job.

He should go back.

Shouldn't he?

He should forget it, drive home. Let sleeping dogs lie. He still had work in the morning. A lot of work.

Yes, just leave it.

An ambulance, lights flashing, went by on the main road. Was it heading towards the accident?

Sod it. He had to know.

If he were careful, he would be fine. It surely couldn't hurt.

He started the car and followed the blue lights.

* * *

A police Astra closed off the road. A police officer in a fluorescent yellow jacket was stopping cars and sending them down a diversion through one of the side streets. Aidan didn't bother to be redirected; he turned down one of the other streets. No point in pushing his luck.

He managed to find a gap in the rows of cars and squeezed the Alfa into the space. He was in front of a boarded up house. On the metal covers over the windows and doors was stencilled the same message over and over again: All items of value removed.

It was not the only house in that state, there were half a dozen; grim and grey and utterly joyless.

Things could certainly only get better.

'Yeah, Tony,' he muttered. 'Good luck with that.'

He locked the car, uttered a silent prayer that it would still be there when he got back and walked towards the accident.

He couldn't get close but no one seemed to be interested in him. That was a plus.

There were three police cars, two ambulances and a fire engine. Their lights illuminated the scene in an unsynchronised symphony of pulsing blue. The ghostly light shone on the faces of the bystanders attracted from their TVs by the free show outside their doors. The light made them appear other-worldish, ghoulish, and hungry for other peoples' suffering to provide them with entertainment.

It made him shudder.

He looked away from the crowd towards the accident.

The two cars had finished some distance apart, the Bentley closest to him. The damage to it was remarkably light given the speed of impact. The offside wing was smashed, the headlights destroyed, the bonnet crumpled and fluid was leaking out from somewhere underneath. The airbags had gone off and hung, white and obscenely flaccid, from the steering wheel.

There was no sign of the driver but the impact looked like one where the occupant would simply walk away shocked, bruised and burnt from the airbags, but otherwise unharmed.

The emergency workers clustered around the other car. What he saw made his stomach tighten.

If he had not seen it before the accident he could not possibly have identified it as a Fiat.

The driver's side had taken the brunt of the impact. He was too far away to see in detail but it looked as though the engine had drove right back into the driver's footwell. Significantly, the fire and ambulance men were ignoring this side of the car and something dark, a coat perhaps, draped over whatever was in there. They were working around the woman in the passenger side.

She wore an oxygen mask, a smear of blood on her cheek. A green-clad paramedic was crouching next to her holding her hand whilst the fireman cut away the metal that trapped her. At that moment, they lifted the roof off, carrying it carefully between four men and putting it to one side.

'Poor thing. She looks proper poorly,' observed one of the women alongside Aidan.

'There's a baby too. Oh the poor lamb,' said someone else. At the car, a paramedic gently cradling a small bundle that was wrapped in a hospital blanket. As he reached the ambulance, the sound of lusty crying reached them, which suggested that there was not too much wrong with the child.

'Bastard who did this should be fuckin' well locked up for life.

'Where is he... er... the driver of the other car?' asked Aidan.

Suddenly he was the focus of the crowd. It seemed that every face turned to look at him with deep suspicion in their eyes.

'Who the fuck are you then?' said a youth with the England top, his eyes wide, his face sneeringly aggressive.

'CID. Narc, that's who he is,' said a freckly, red-haired boy who looked about twelve. Aidan felt the hostility rising.

'I'm not a cop,' he said. 'I'm a reporter. I was just passing and saw the blue lights.'

The lie almost stuck in his throat.

'Yeah, right, 'course you are,' said the woman.

Aidan took out his wallet, extracted his press pass and showed it to the woman. She squinted at it through piggy eyes in a way that suggested that she needed reading glasses. The red-haired boy elbowed rudely in, stuck out a grubby hand, and grasped the card. There was a brief tug of war before Aidan won.

'You pay for stories then?' said the woman.

'No. Well not usually but...'

The sound of revving power tool drew the crowd's attention. They'd lost interest in Aidan. He was not going to get anywhere with them so he left the crowd and tried to get closer to the Fiat.

He managed to get right up to the officer operating the diversion, around fifty metres from the Fiat. Two firemen were working down in the passenger footwell, one with his torso inside the car. The sound of a hacksaw blade on metal. The other held a floodlight and shone it into the void. The paramedic was still holding the woman's hand and was talking reassuringly to her, telling her that she was doing fine, that the baby was OK and that she would soon be out. The woman looked to be in her early twenties. She had long, straight, mousy hair, her eyes held the look of a frightened, cornered animal. Beyond the girl, he could see a hand protruding out from under the coat laid over the driver's remains. A trickle of blood ran down the hand and drip, dripped into the darkness of the footwell and onto the remains of the gearstick.

Aidan felt sick again. He'd been part of this. He was responsible. Partly at least.

The fireman holding the light looked up into Aidan's eyes. There was look of pure contempt on the man's face.

For a moment he almost panicked, almost ran. Then common sense took over; he can't know, he just thinks I'm a rubbernecker. Still he'd seen enough. He turned and walked away.

It was then he saw him.

One of the police cars parked on the side of the road suddenly illuminated from within. Someone must have cracked open one of the doors and the courtesy light had come on. It revealed a handcuffed man sat in the back seat of the car whilst two officers sat in the front.

It was the driver, he recognised him despite only glimpsing him in the moment before the crash.

Aidan wasn't sure what he was expecting him to look like. A businessman perhaps; but not this.

He was short, stocky and powerful. He looked like a bouncer, someone you'd see outside a pub or club.

Well, whatever, he'd been arrested and rightly so. Aidan hoped they threw the book at him.

Heartened by this sight, but not wanting to be seen by the man in case he recognised Aidan in turn, he continued to make his way back to the Alfa.

Deja vu. Headlights, blindingly bright, Xenon headlights were coming down the street towards him. He stepped back into the shadows as another Bentley passed him driving slowly, clearly looking for somewhere to park.

His curiosity was now piqued. This had to be more than a coincidence. Two top-of-the-range limos around here? Not a coincidence, surely they had to come from the same place? If so then the psychopathic driver had to have real power and money. So who was he? A footballer? No, too old. How about a manager or a football agent then? If not that then somebody in the media? Something vaguely familiar about him niggled at Aidan. Was he an actor? He was not an avid soap watcher but it was almost impossible not to get some exposure to them. Had he seen him on one of those and his memory been triggered?

This meant that there might be a story here and a big one at that. Moreover, he was in the right place at the right time, whatever the circumstances.

Aidan turned back the way he had come, following the Bentley.

It soon stopped. There was nowhere to park with the end of the street now blocked by the ambulance. The rear door opened; there were two men inside, both looking down the road. The driver was in a grey suit, he had a peaked cap on. A chauffeur.

Interesting. More confirmation that there was serious wealth involved here.

Aidan stepped back into the shadows. Not many of the street lamps were working; probably because people objected to them shining into their bedroom windows Aidan surmised. Anyway, at least it gave him some cover.

The rear door of the Bentley opened fully and the passengers stepped out. Again, they were not at all what Aidan expected, certainly not some high-powered executives. One was a lean bald man, mean looking, in a white t-shirt and leather jacket. The other nondescript figure was fair-haired, his receding hairline giving him a distinct widow's peak. His weedy build, gaunt face and pale weak mouth, was dressed in cheap jeans with a creased blue polo shirt.

This was getting increasingly odd.

After a few further moments of discussion - instruction - the nondescript blond man set off towards the accident, passing close by Aidan as he did. Aidan got an odd aroma, or at least particularly odd here in a city centre; it was of horse, definitely a horsey smell, manure, straw and sweat. Strange.

More than curious now, he followed, keeping in the shadows where possible. The man pushed through the bystanders and walked straight up to the first police officer who put a hand up to stop him. He turned an ear towards the man, obviously struggling to hear him over the noise of the power tools sawing through the Fiat.

His puzzled expression changed. Without replying to the man, the police officer led him over to the patrol car, which held the driver. The front passenger window wound down and the man leaned in to talk to the two officers inside.

'What the hell does he think he's going to achieve?' Aidan muttered to himself.

To his astonishment, one of the policemen reached over into the back of the car and undid the handcuffs. The other got out and opened the rear door. The driver got out, rubbing his wrists whilst the two policemen returned to their seats.

There was a jeer from the crowd, an almost primal hiss of disapproval. A shout.

The newly released man ignored it. He was talking to the fair-haired man who listened, nodded and then moved towards the nearest police officer. It was not a long conversation; in fact, it looked very much like an order. The blond man moved off, this time back to the first police officer who was back facing the crowd again, doing his duty by keeping them back. And this time the driver came with him. The policeman listened again and nodded. He then walked towards the crowd, the driver and the blond man following.

'Step back there, out of the way,' he said. 'I need to get this gentleman through.'

'What the fucks 'appening?' said the woman. 'Why you taken the cuffs off 'im?'

'That's none of your business, now step back,' said the policeman.

The second Bentley waiting in the street moved smoothly forward.

'They're fuckin' lettin' 'im go!' yelled the England shirted youth. 'What the fuck you done that for?' He looked wild eyed and dangerous.

'Watch your language, son, or I'll nick you,' the officer said threateningly.

'Cummon' Fed, what you gonna do then?' the youth spat at the nearest cop.

'Right, you!' said the policeman drawing his baton and extending it 'Back up!' he shouted over over his shoulder.

He dived at the youth. In the commotion the distracted crowd missed the driver, the bald minder and the blond man get into the Bentley – the driver in the back, the blond man alongside the chauffeur – and the car rapidly reverse off down the street suggesting a highly skilled, tactically trained driver.

Aidan didn't miss it, he watched, open-mouthed.

Extracted from the wreck back at the Fiat, the woman was stretchered into the ambulance. Three officers had jumped on the youth and were pinning him to the tarmac. Others moved in to keep the hostile crowd at bay.

In a daze, Aidan walked back to his car.

Chapter Three

May 2nd 1997, 8.55am

Aidan was late and feeling like death. He wasn't inclined to go easy on himself; his condition was self-inflicted.

On the way home, passing the late-night shop near his flat he craved a stiff drink to calm his nerves. He'd stopped and bought a bottle of vodka and a mixer.

He would have one, just one and then go to bed.

He'd had three hefty ones and was paying for it.

He'd slept through his alarm then, waking forty minutes later and after having a hot shower, tried to force down some toast in the vague hope that putting something in his stomach would ease his hangover. Instead, it had rasped his already tender throat on the way down and then sunk to his stomach like a brick. He'd watched the breakfast news whilst eating, full of Major resigning, Cherie Blair being caught looking rough opening the door in her night things, only half listened to the talking heads analysing the results. He should care, it would affect the business world big time but his mind was elsewhere.

In his state he really shouldn't be in at all; ordinarily he probably wouldn't but, given what had happened, he needed to project a 'business as usual' persona just in case the police came looking for him. He'd resolved to brazen it out if they did, to deny all knowledge.

He walked boldly into the office and navigated his way to his desk, sure that every eye was on him and that they could smell the vodka oozing out of his pores. He made it to his desk, slumped into his chair and switched his computer on. Whilst it booted up, Aidan tried to boot himself awake.

The computer started up quickly. He didn't.

Despite his lateness, he'd still beaten Richard in.

That was no real surprise; Richard marched to the beat of his own drum, worked to his own schedule, came in when he wanted, and yet this seemed to satisfy the editors. Why? It was obvious: because he kept producing good stories. Aidan was envious of Richard's freedom but it was undeniable that, just occasionally, Richard found an earth-shattering story that no one else, no rival journalist, no other paper, not even the nationals had gotten a sniff of it. There was no regular output of these exclusives nor in their subjects. It was a bit like major earthquakes; the big ones came infrequently and in familiar but unpredictable places, but when they happened the earth moved.

It was another twenty minutes before Richard arrived. He strolled in looking as he always did: rumpled, crumpled, and totally unconcerned, at ease with the world and comfortable in his own rather flabby skin. He carried something that's aroma mugged Aidan's senses; A coffee in a tall takeaway cup.

'Is that a fresh coffee?' Aidan muttered.

Richard took a sip and smiled. 'A black with a double shot espresso,' he said. 'Want to split it?'

'Please.'

'Pass us your mug.'

Aidan picked it up, the last third of yesterday afternoon's tea still in the bottom which he tipped into the nearest pot plant before handing it over. He watched with hungry eyes as Richard poured half of his coffee into it.

The hot liquid burnt his lips but the caffeine started to work its magic almost instantly. Richard watched with an amused look on his face.

'Rough night?' he said.

'You could say that.'

'I thought you were heading home? You'd already had a

skinful. What on earth possessed you to go somewhere else?'

'I didn't, I drank more at home.'

'Drowning your sorrows after the election? Didn't have you down as a Tory.'

'It wasn't because of that,' he glanced around then lowered his voice. 'Richard, I've messed up, I really have. There was this accident, not me, not really, another couple of cars but it was bad, someone died, at least I think they did, and I was sort of involved,' he swallowed. 'I just drove off. I left them to it.'

Richard stared at him, and then shook his head.

'You were driving? After what we put away?'

'Yes, I know.'

'You bloody idiot. It's usually me that does stupid stuff like that.'

'I know, but...'

'But what?'

'It wasn't the accident that shook me. It was what happened afterward.'

'What do you mean afterward?'

'I went back, not to hand myself in but to check, you know, see if everyone was all right.'

'Which they weren't.'

'No. But something really strange happened.'

'Strange? What?'

Aidan took another sip of coffee. The caffeine was really kicking in now; the fog in his brain was clearing. Yes, this was Richard, yes, he was a mate but he was also a reporter, a bloody good one. It was helping talking to someone but he really should keep things to himself.

'It was nothing. Forget it,' he said.

Richard shook his head. 'I can't now, can I? Come on, Aidan wake up. It's not going to take me long if I start digging, which I will. I'll find out about it, you know that, it's what I do,' he stared intently at Aidan. 'You might as well tell me.'

Aidan knew he was right, so did, in as much detail as he could remember. Richard listened intently without interrupting.

'Now that is interesting,' he said. 'There was no chance of the police mistaking whose fault it was?'

'No way. The Bentley was on the wrong side of the road. The Fiat was on its own side. They'd have to be blind to think otherwise.'

Richard nodded thoughtfully. 'Who the hell has that sort of clout?'

Aidan could see he was hooked, he'd seen that look a few times before; it was Richard's terrier look; he would not let go now, he'd keep worrying the story until he got to the bottom of it.

Richard turned back to his desk, picked up his phone and punched in three numbers; internal then, thought Aidan.

'Suzie? It's Richard. Hi, how you doing? Yes, I know, long time. Of course I haven't forgotten you, how could I?'

That had to be Suzie Regan, a protégé of Richard's and one who he was once rumoured to have had a very close relationship with indeed. Suzie was on the news desk. Aidan had always given her a wide berth, finding her intense and quite scary.

'So how you doing, love? Brilliant... yeah, I'm fine, same as ever. Yeah, I know what fine means! Look Suzie, did someone cover the RTA in Salford last night? About half eleven, twelve o'clock?' He looked at Aidan for confirmation about the time; he nodded. 'Yes... who was it? Sophie? Do I know her? Oh right... yeah, I know the one.' He laughed, 'Yeah, well you know me. Anyway, what did she say? A Bentley parked with its lights on? The other car ploughed into it. The Bentley driver released without charge. Right... any names? Yeah, the driver of the Fiat. Bloody hell, can you spell that?' Richard wrote the name out. 'Sounds Polish? Yeah, probably, there's a lot over here. And the other driver...' he waited. 'She's not got it? That's unusual isn't it? She did try? Well yes, I thought she would, you'll be training her well. So the police wouldn't release it? Well, well, well.' He listened to what Suzie was saying, 'No love, I don't know who it was. No... look, honest I don't. Of course I would let you know if there was a story.' He rolled his eyes at Aidan. 'OK Suze, gotta go. Yes I will! Bye.'

He put the phone down and puffed out his cheeks. 'Bloody hell. she's a nightmare. Just like me, I guess.' he looked at Aidan. 'You got the gist of that?'

'Yeah, I think so.'

'There's something funny going on here. Did you get the number of the Bentley?'

Aidan's heart sank. 'No,' he admitted. 'Sorry. I don't think I ever actually saw it.'

Richard grimaced. 'Shame that. I wonder if I know any of the cops on the scene? They might know it. It'll be a hell of a job to ring round though.'

Aidan wracked his brains. What a fool, what sort of reporter was he? Surely that was basic, he should have got the registration number. Then a thought hit him.

'I remember the number of the other Bentley, the one the blond man came in.' He scribbled it down and passed it to Richard who took it triumphantly.

He turned back to his desk and pulled out his little black contact book. He would never let this leave his side nor would he change it to an electronic version, it was too valuable. Aidan often found himself wishing that he had the same level of contacts. Richard found the number he was looking for and punched it into his phone.

'Hi Carole. It's Richard Tasker. How are you?'

Another woman, Aidan thought. Of course.

'Yeah, yeah, I'm fine. No, no one special at the moment... anyway, I thought you were happily married?' He laughed, a rich, gentle laugh. 'Yeah right, I believe you. Look, Carole I'm after a favour. Yeah, I DO want to talk to you anyway. I promise I'll take you out, husband or no husband... yeah, somewhere expensive. Look, I want you to check a car reg for me... yeah, I know you shouldn't but it's just for me. It'll go no further... brilliant, you're a honey.' He winked at Aidan as he read out the car registration, 'OK, thanks. Can you spell that? A, S, T, C, A, N, Z, A. Astcanza, that right? Astcanza Limited. OK brilliant, you're an angel... I'll call you... yes soon! Bye Carole.'

He put the phone down. Aidan realised that the woman must have access to the police vehicle databases. Again he asked himself how Richard did it.

Richard held out the post-it note he'd written the company name on. Aidan took it.

'Astcanza Limited. Mean anything to you?'

Before Aidan could answer his phone rang.

'Aidan Hughes?' he said.

'Aidan, where the hell have you been?' His heart sank; it was Gill, the editor.

'Gill. Yes, I'm sorry about...'

'Where were you? I've been ringing your extension for an hour and your mobile is off.'

'Is it? I was...'

'Where's the post-election analysis? The one I told you I wanted first thing today.'

'It's... er... coming.'

'It bloody well better had be. Within the hour, Aidan. On my desk.'

She rang off.

'Oh dear, that didn't sound good,' said Richard in a mock-solemn tone. 'Don't worry, happens to me all the time.'

Aidan passed the post-it note back and turned disconsolately to his keyboard. The election. He'd forgotten all about it. What the hell could he cobble together?

'Look,' said Richard, 'It looks like you're going to be tied up for a while. Do you mind if I dig around this accident story? I've got time.'

Aidan sighed. He did mind, this was his story, but what choice did he have? 'Be my guest.'

'Great!' said Richard and looked at his watch. 'Well I'm not going to get far here. I'm going to see a few people, see what they know. Catch you later.'

With that he went.

A new record thought Aidan. Ten minutes, max, in the office. How did he get away with it?

He turned to his blank screen.

Hell, why would he get himself involved in this?

* * *

Aidan left the office at 7pm, tired but relieved.

Firstly he hadn't had a call from the police. It looked like he'd got away with it. Secondly, he'd successfully submitted his article. It was a bit derivative and rather general. Gill had looked at it carefully, made a few very minor amendments – probably just for show – but had grudgingly accepted it. That was enough for him, he wasn't after a Pulitzer prize. He then buckled down to his normal tasks, knowing that he had only half the time that he would normally have to get it done. Oddly, his tiredness seemed to redouble his energy and helped him focus on work and not the normal peripheral distractions, and he finished far earlier than he thought he would.

He knew that he would pay for this boost later and, indeed, sitting on the tram on the way home he felt himself nodding off. He almost slept through his stop, getting off just in time. Aidan couldn't be bothered to cook so picked up a Chinese from his local takeaway, the banquet for one meant that he didn't have to expend the mental effort of choosing.

As he was turning the key in the door his mobile rang. Briefly juggling Chinese, keys and phone he at last got the latter to his ear.

'Hello?' he said.

'Aidan? Where are you? It's me.' Aidan could hear music in the background, a babble of voices, laughter.

'Where do you think I am, Richard? I'm at home.'

'What you doing there? I thought you'd be at the pub.'

'Not after last night. Anyway, work today was a nightmare. For those who could be bothered to be in, of course.'

Aidan heard a bleep on the line and a muffled curse.

'Sod it. The battery's going. Look, can you get down here?'

'No I bloody can't. I've just picked up a Chinese. I'm going to eat it then hit the sack.'

He would normally have been more diplomatic, but he was tired and irritable beyond measure.

'Oh. Right. OK. Sorry.' There was a pause. 'It's not just for a drink though.'

Aidan had put the Chinese down on the kitchen worktop and had prised the lid off the spareribs. His mouth watered at the prospect of the sticky-sweet meat. Richard's words hit home though.

'What do you mean, the story?'

'Yup, it's the story. You wouldn't believe it. It's big, mate.' The bleep went again. 'Shit, this is going. Look, it doesn't matter. I can tell you all about it in the morning. I forgot about the crap night you had.'

Aidan was interested now though and fully awake again.

'I could get down. I'd be an hour or so though.'

'Don't worry. I'm meeting someone in twenty minutes so-'

The line went dead.

'Richard? Richard?' Aidan knew it was futile but tried ringing back. The number was unobtainable.

It was typical of Richard; he was always forgetting to charge his phone.

He thought about leaving his Chinese and heading out to find Richard. He must be calling from their usual watering hole. But if he moved on, without his mobile, Aidan stood very little chance of finding him.

His curiosity was in overdrive though; what had Richard found out?

He picked up a spare-rib and bit into it. Nectar, pure, guilty pleasure.

Decision made: He grabbed a fork and a plate and went into the lounge, putting the TV on.

He fell asleep about an hour later in front of a film and didn't wake until the early hours when he dragged himself off to bed.

He intended to sleep most of the weekend.

Though he also needed to find a garage to MOT and repair his car.

* * *

MONDAY MORNING, May 5th, 1997, 8.45am

Late again.

He could not believe he'd overslept. He should learn to get up with the alarm and not press snooze. He couldn't risk the wrath of Gill; she was bound to see him sneaking in late. Push it once too often and he'd be out.

He was irritated that he'd still beaten Richard in. He'd tried to ring him over the weekend a couple of times but it had gone straight to voicemail. And now he was late in again, damn him. He wanted to find out what he'd discovered that had got him so excited. He could also do with a coffee hit; he was sure that Richard would bring another one in, he usually did.

Aidan settled down to work. There were rumours that Gordon Brown was going to announce something big shortly. He needed to ring around to see if anyone had a heads up of what it might be.

He became quite engrossed and therefore jumped when Gill

spoke. She was standing right next to him.

'This is his desk,' she said.

She wasn't alone. There was a man with her, dark suited, white shirt, sober tie, late twenties or early thirties, fit and trim.

Aidan recognised the type: Police.

Shit, they'd found him.

'Right, thank you. It may help, we have to try to clear up the loose ends. He may have left a note or there perhaps there'ssomething else on it that might explain what happened. Any objection to me having a quick look?' he said.

He sat down at Richard's desk. Aidan breathed a sigh of relief. He hadn't come for him, it was Richard.

'So what the hell has the old sod done this time?' he said.

Gill's reaction was not what he expected; she went pale and was suddenly not the confident competent woman that Aidan knew so well. Something was wrong.

'What is it? What's happened to Richard?'

She took a deep breath, clearly steeling herself.

'You've got to know. Everyone will soon anyway,' she said. 'Richard is dead. It looks like suicide. He jumped off the City Tower just after midnight on Friday.'

Chapter Four

Gill's words were clear but Aidan struggled to process their meaning. The others around him must have been the same for the entire office had fallen silent.

'Suicide?' he said at last.

'It seems so.'

'That can't be. I talked to him that night. He was fine.'

'You spoke to him? What time was this?'

The policeman pulled out his notebook

Aidan looked questioningly at Gill but the policeman got there first. 'DS Franks,' he said tersely, 'and you are?'

'Aidan Hughes.'

'You knew Mr Tasker well?'

Franks was waiting expectantly with pen poised.

'I worked with him for two, no…no, three years. We used to go drinking together after work. Sometimes, anyway.'

Often, thought Aidan, probably too bloody often actually. And then it hit him; used to, not any more. A leaden, hollow feeling formed deep in the pit of his stomach.

'What time did you speak to him? Was this in person? Or on the phone?'

Franks was being brusque to the point of rudeness, his tone almost accusatory. Was he deliberately rubbing Aidan the wrong way?

'On the phone.'

'And what time was this?'

'About seven I guess. No later, about seven thirty, I suppose.'

'You can't be more precise?'

'No I can't.'

He hoped the coldness in his voice got his feelings across.

Franks stared at Aidan for a few moments as if expecting something more. Aidan stared back.

'What did you talk about?'

Aidan hesitated. He should tell what he knew.

But how could he? How could he explain about the story Richard was pursuing, his excitement about what he'd found, without mentioning the accident? He was taking too long but just couldn't think and the moments stretched into full, awkward, suspicious seconds.

Franks sighed. 'Mr Hughes, I'd advise you not to keep anything back that would assist us with our investigations.'

Officious prick, thought Aidan, and he decided to say nothing.

'He just wanted me to go for a drink, that's all. I was already back at my flat with a Chinese.'

Franks' brow furrowed. 'That's it? Nothing else?'

'No,' said Aidan firmly.

'Was he with anyone?'

'Not as far as I know.'

'He wasn't,' said Dev, one of the other reporters. The policeman swung around to look at him, Dev now got the staring treatment. He stirred in his seat, clearly uncomfortable although, obviously, he had no reason to be.

'I was in the pub. I saw him. In fact I saw him on the phone. He wasn't with anyone else.'

'And he looked and sounded completely normal?'

'Yeah, completely. Bloody Hell, Richard's dead! I can't believe it.'

Franks jotted down the information from Dev, taking his name and address first. Aidan's mind wandered. The same thought kept running through his head. Could there be any connection between the accident and Richard's death?

'Are you sure it was suicide? Someone didn't just push him

off the roof?'

A few moments later he realised Franks and Dev had stopped talking and all eyes had turned towards him. Hell, in his tiredness he'd just blurted out his thoughts.

'And why would you say that Mr Hughes?' Franks face was impassive but his gaze was unrelenting. 'Is there something you want to tell us?'

'No, no. It's just that Richard wasn't the suicidal type. I just can't imagine him jumping that's all'

The policeman's eyes bored into him. A staring contest, eh, thought Aidan, bring it on. He fought to keep calm.

Franks broke off first. He sat down at Richard's desk and picked up the mouse.

The moment had been broken. A minor victory. And sod you, thought Aidan, I'm not a bloody suspect.

'Going back to your conversation with Mr Tasker,' Franks said without looking up at Aidan. 'How did he seem to you?'

'Perfectly normal. Typically Richard.'

'Not down at all? Depressed?'

'Richard depressed? Come on! Richard was never down.'

Franks raised his eyebrows. 'We found large doses of Fluoxetine at his flat.'

Aidan looked blankly at the policeman.

'It's a brand of Prozac. Antidepressants? You didn't know?'

Anti-depressants? Richard? Bloody hell.

'No,' he said, quietly.

Franks nodded and turned back to the screen. He clicked the mouse a few times.

'That's odd,' he said.

'What?'

'There's nothing on here.'

'What do you mean nothing?' said Gill.

'I mean nothing. Nothing at all. No files, no recent work. It's like the computer is new. A blank.'

'That can't be,' said Gill stepping closer and tilting her head back to look through her reading glasses.

'Are these files backed up on the intranet?' Franks was clearly a technophile. Aidan had a feeling that was why he had been sent.

'Anything that we save on the H, J and K drives are yes but work in progress and private files are saved locally on the C. It's not supposed to be done but everyone works that way. They only get saved to the server if people pass them across into another drive. This is crazy, you're right, there's absolutely nothing.'

'Has anyone else got access to his machine?' Franks looked at Aidan but addressed his question to Gill.

'Not that I'm aware of.' Gill also looked at Aidan who was getting increasingly conscious of the attention.

'Richard worked alone,' he said. 'He could be quite secretive at times. And you haven't answered my question; it was suicide wasn't it? Do you have any reason to suspect that it wasn't?'

Franks hesitated. Aidan wondered whether he was trying to draw Aidan into some kind of trap, to invite him to fill in the silence by saying something, something that might later be used against him. He was not going to oblige. He waited and his patience was rewarded.

'No. We have no particular reason to consider anything but suicide. We have a CCTV tape from the hotel that shows Mr Tasker go up to the roof on his own. No one else was up there with him.'

'Right, so-'

We are obliged to investigate every sudden death thoroughly.'

'Of course,' said Gill. 'And we will, naturally, do everything in our power to assist you in those investigations.'

'In the circumstances that's what we'd expect.' Again his gaze was fixed on Aidan. Why couldn't he pick on someone else, why had he fixated on him? 'In the meantime, did Mr Tasker have a mobile and laptop?'

'Not a laptop, he wouldn't have one, too old school, but a

phone, yes. And his notebook of course.'

'A notebook?' Franks made a note in his own.

'Of course. Essential tools of the trade. Why, haven't you found it?'

'No. They weren't on his body.'

'They were probably in his car,' said Aidan. 'What about his contact book? He was never without that.'

Franks shook his head. 'No, he had nothing like that. And we found his car this morning parked on Liverpool Street on an expired meter, it came up on the DVLC so we knew it was his and already had his keys which we'd recovered from the body. There was no notebook, no contact book, no phone.'

A long silence following the delivery of this bombshell.

'That is strange,' sighed Gill. 'Mind you, it all is.'

'That's why we have to keep an open mind,' said Franks. 'We're not going to rush to a judgement on this. We're going to investigate this fully. I trust everyone will give us their complete assistance.' Again, although Franks eyes scanned the room they ended up on Aidan and lingered on him longest.

'Of course. What can we do to help?' said Gill.

'I'll need to take some statements. Is there an office I can use?'

'Certainly. I'll arrange one of the meeting rooms to be put at your disposal. I'd give you my office but I still have a paper to get out.' Like most editors, Gill always gave the impression of doing everything herself. 'If you'd like to follow me?'

Whilst Gill led the policeman away in the direction of the meeting rooms the buzz of conversation rose all around him. Aidan himself wanted to shut it out. He swivelled around in his chair and tried to focus on his screen. It was impossible because Richard's face kept swimming into view and the same question kept coming back to him again and again.

Why had he kept back the information about what Richard was looking into?

He couldn't find a proper answer.

Chapter Five

Gill leaned out of her office door.

'Aidan, would you come in here a second?' she said.

'What now?' he muttered to himself under his breath.

He was surprised to see Trevor Jones, the paper's head of security, in the office with her, a laptop open on the desk in front of him.

'What's up?' he said with a quizzical glance towards Trevor.

'Life has got to go on, I'm afraid, we still have to put the paper out. You're going to have to take on Richard's job for the time being. What was the big announcement from the Treasury? Something or nothing?'

'Something. He's given the Bank of England independence to set rates.'

Gill nodded. 'Interesting. We'll need a piece on that. Oh and the quarterly property market report is due isn't it? Are you okay with doing that?'

'Yes, of course.'

That still didn't explain Trevor's presence.

'So ideally you'll need the files that used to be held on Richard's computer, won't you?'

'Oh yes, I will. Have you asked IT to try and recover them?'

'They're still trying to. But I asked for the security tapes from last night to be brought up to see if we could see who tampered with Richard's computer,' she said. 'Trevor, would you mind showing Aidan?'

'Certainly. This is what we found on the disk.' He clicked the mouse and the video started playing on the screen. It was rather poor quality, grainy, typical security footage showing different views of parts of the office building. By the look of things there were three cameras. Aidan had always been vaguely aware of their existence, it was one of the features of working in a 24 hour office; it had to be there for their safety and security. The images were switching from one to another view, probably as part of an automatic setting; it moved from the lift, to the right side of the office, then to the left where Aidan's and Richard's desk was located.

'I just extracted the right section from the master files and burned them to this disk,' said Jones. The man had a habit of wearing huge amounts of cheap deodorant and Aidan was very aware of this as he leaned over him. He noticed that Gill was keeping her distance, but then she had presumably already viewed the videos.

'Look there.' Jones pointed at the screen where a view of the lift lobby was currently being displayed. A man had just stepped out of one of the lifts. He paused as if unsure of where he was going. That could not be right though because this man should know exactly where he was going.

It was Richard.

'What time was this shot?' said Aidan.

'Just after midnight,' said Jones pointing to the time stamp.

On the screen, Richard walked across the room to his desk, not acknowledging anyone. They watched in silence as Richard sat down at his desk and turned his computer on. He then spent several minutes clicking his mouse and typing something into his keyboard. The cameras seemed to be on a fifteen second cycle. They went back to Richard three times then, on the fourth, his desk was empty. The camera by the lift picked him up waiting in the lobby. At the next cycle he was gone.

'That was it? No one else went to his workstation?' said Aidan.

'No. That was all there was,' said Jones.

'Richard wiped the computer himself?'

'You sound surprised,' said Gill.

'I am. He wasn't very computer savvy. I'm surprised he knew how to do it.'

'IT said he did a pretty thorough job.'

'But we had to help him to do all but the simplest things.'

'That's what I thought,' she said. 'And why do it anyway if he was going to commit suicide?' Gill raised a quizzical eyebrow 'That's why you're here. You knew him best. You worked with him. Why would he wipe his files?'

Aidan swallowed. 'I don't know.'

Gill showed no sign of believing him.

'I had a strong feeling you were holding something back from DS Franks. Were you?'

So, now he had to tell a direct lie. He was better prepared than when Franks had asked him.

'No, I wasn't. I was just in shock. I really don't know.'

Wanting to move things on Aidan asked, 'Have the police seen these?'

'No. I wanted to have a look at them before we passed them on. The last thing we need is footage of someone snorting something they shouldn't on camera. Why?'

'No reason. I just wondered.'

'Well I suppose we'd better get this to them. There's no reason not to.' She looked at the screen again and shook her head. 'Oh Richard, why didn't you come to us if you were having problems?'

The question hung in the air but it was clear that the interview was over and that they should leave. 'Trevor, please courier the footage to the police please.'

'Certainly, Mrs Phillips.'

Aidan went back to his desk and tried to lose himself in work. He still had deadlines to meet, life had to go on. People around him seemed to be letting him get on with things, in fact they gave him a wide berth. Why? Did they think he was lying too?

Whatever. It allowed him to get stuff done and also gave him time to think.

To think about that key question: should he act on what he knew or forget it?

He should leave the whole thing well alone; if there was a story and Richard had uncovered something, then he'd died for it. Aidan was not ready to die just yet.

But it wasn't enough. Something was bothering him. He needed to know.

When Richard was in the office he was alone. When he was on the roof of City Tower he was alone. But did he arrive at either building that way?

Something told him he hadn't.

Leave it.

It was the sensible thing to do.

But Aidan was not sensible.

He left his desk taking the stairs down two floors to the little windowless cubbyhole that was Trevor's realm. To Aidan's relief he was still there.

'Mr Hughes. Can I help?'

Trevor must have renewed his deodorant or else it was stronger for having another hour to develop. Whatever, it was almost overpowering in the confined space.

'I was just curious about something. We have cameras outside the building don't we?'

'Yes. Over the main entrance and the fire escapes.'

'Could I be a pain and look at the tapes for just before midnight?'

Trevor frowned but said, 'yes, of course. I've just been backing the files up. They should be on this disk.' He picked up a CD-RW and put it into the drive of the computer on his desk. He then selected a time period and an image appeared on the screen. It was the entrance of the building taken from above and looking down at a fairly sharp angle. Trevor played the video through at quadruple speed from 11.30 pm. There were, not surprisingly given the hour, very few comings and goings. Even with a 24 hour office, night time was still the graveyard shift.

'There!' said Aidan suddenly – and unnecessarily because Trevor had already paused the playback and was rewinding back. He played the video again, this time at the normal speed. It was Richard. He had paused outside of the entrance. Again there was that sense he was momentarily confused and it took a few moments to actually go inside.

'Is that what you wanted to see?' said Trevor.

'Er yes... thanks. Is it all right if...?' he indicated the mouse that was in the hands of the security man.

'Of course,' he said, passing it over.

Aidan paused the video and ran it backwards and forwards several times, stepping through a few frames at a time. The quality was not brilliant and he had to step it through four or five times before he was sure: Before Richard had stepped into frame his shadow thrown by the streetlight out of shot had preceded him.

But it wasn't just a single shadow, it was two.

Richard hadn't been alone. The other person had hung back and let Richard go inside. Then they remained standing there, waiting, just out of view.

'So who the hell are you?' said Aidan under his breath.

Chapter Six

Aiden needed a drink after work but, whilst the others had gathered for an unofficial wake for Richard at the paper's usual watering hole, he wanted to be alone so chose a different pub.

And to think about the story.

But what story? There was only one obvious one: Richard had found a tall building and had stepped off it to his personal oblivion. Period. Yes, he'd done something odd, gone back to the office and wiped everything but, if you'd got so desperate that you were going to do something like throwing yourself off a tall building, acting oddly was to be expected.

Wasn't it?

Wouldn't he do the same? Perhaps he should, he thought; his life was pretty shitty after all.

With difficulty he dragged himself away from these morbid and dangerous thoughts.

Back to the story.

A big story. That's what Richard had said. Aidan hadn't seen him so excited in years.

This was Aidan's dream. A big story that would make his name, the one he'd always longed for.

His Watergate.

His lottery ticket.

But what was it? Had it died with Richard? Maybe, but whilst it could have been coincidence that Richard had chosen to kill himself the very day that he had started to investigate, that was surely pushing credibility far too far.

There had to be a link, but what?

Richard had jumped alone, at least going on what the police said. There was no evidence of murder from the hotel CCTV.

Open and shut.

But he was also alone when he was wiping his hard drive but was not alone when he arrived at the building. The owner of the mysterious second shadow showed that. And where was his notebook and mobile? And his little black book, the one that never left his person.

Who had them?

Shit, whoever had them would have Aidan's address, that was in there. They would have found references to Aidan in Richard's notebook. As soon as they recharged Richard's phone they'd have seen that Aidan was the last person he'd called.

They'd know all about him.

If they'd killed Richard they'd be coming for him.

'God, you look miserable. Let's hope it was some girl that stood you up for a change.'

The voice that cut through his thoughts wasn't unpleasant, in fact quite the reverse; rich, warm, female with a southern Irish accent, though the delivery was mocking. Aidan knew it well. He looked up into the bright green eyes of Roisin Malone.

'Hi, Roisin,' he said, 'You alright?'

'My feet are killing me but not too bad. You?'

They had met in the same place, at this same table about a year ago, dated for a few months, until she'd got bored of Aidan's excuses, guessing - correctly - that he was frightened about commitment.

He wasn't guessing at her reasons for ending it; she'd told him. In no uncertain terms she'd made it quite clear why it was over. It had been a shock, nonetheless.

'I've been better,' he said.

She smiled, 'Oh, good.'

He frowned, shocked for a moment. Then he realised.

'You haven't heard, have you?'

'Heard? Heard what? It's peak time. I've not had a moment.'

He steeled himself for what he was about to say, not just because Richard and Roisin had got on well but because he had never actually said the words before, like until he actually uttered them it wasn't real.

And when he did it was like driving the nails into the coffin lid.

'Richard's dead. He jumped off the City Tower in the early hours of Saturday morning.'

He saw the words hit home.

'The man who jumped. That was Richard?' Roisin sank onto a vacant stool. 'Oh my God, we were talking about it in the shop.'

'Yes. Do you need a drink?' he said getting to his feet.

'Shit, we joked about it, said that was one refund we wouldn't have to give.' she shook her head then realised Aidan was waiting. 'Yeah, a Bacardi and Coke. A big one.'

Aidan left her and went to the bar. Drink might not be the solution but it was helping. For the first time today he had started to feel better. He took the drinks back to the table and handed Roisin hers.

'Thanks,' she said. 'Why did he do it? Do they know?'

'I don't know,' he said. 'He seemed fine the last time I saw him.'

'Wait, I saw him,' said Roisin suddenly, 'Friday night! I was in here. I wouldn't have known anything was wrong. He looked... well excited, how he always did when he was pleased with himself, you know?'

'Like he looked when he was onto a big story?' said Aidan.

'Yes. Yes, exactly like that,' Roisin stared at Aidan. 'You don't think this makes sense either, do you?'

Aidan sighed. 'No I don't. But everything else points at suicide.'

'I can't believe it,' said Roisin shaking her head again, 'We could see the police outside the building, saw them on the roof. And that was Richard. I never knew, I never knew.'

It suddenly hit him.

Roisin had seen the police from her shop.

Roisin managed a travel agents, it was virtually opposite City Tower. God, was this the answer to his big question? 'I'd forgotten your shop was down there,' he said.

'You forget a lot of things. You always did.'

Aidan tried to ignore the waspish barb.

'Does it have CCTV?' he asked as casually as he could.

* * *

May 5th 1997 9.45pm

'I can't believe you've got me doing this,' grumbled Roisin, 'I should be home with a bottle of vino watching the box.'

'It's for Richard,' said Aidan trying to suppress his guilt.

'Yeah, right, 'course it is.'

They were in the storeroom-cum-office-cum-staffroom at the back of the agency and Roisin was leaning over the CCTV monitor. Unlike the paper's, this one was extremely ancient using VHS tapes but the images they produced were reasonably clear, better than the ones at the office.

'You want the night tape, the one on the outside camera?'

'Yup, Thursday night... well, Friday morning really. It was after midnight.'

She selected a tape from the box underneath the table.

'You're in luck. I have been known to forget to switch them over and just record over them.'

'How long do they last?'

'They're four hour tapes set to run a double time giving eight hours.'

Aidan did the calculation in his head. 'So they actually run out in the middle of the night?'

Roisin gave an embarrassed smile. 'Good company you know, this one. Nothing but the best for us.'

She inserted the tape into the machine and pressed fast forward. Aidan heard the tape spool and rattle forward, wondering how many times it had been used and whether it would stand up to this treatment. He remembered the video tapes from his childhood, how brittle and fragile they got with age. He winced as Roisin pressed play on the machine whilst it was still running forward. It worked though, the image flickered onto the screen. She pressed rewind without stopping it; Aidan visualised the delicate brown tape stretching then breaking with the punishment. The counter and time stamp wound back though. People could be seen walking backwards, comically quickly. One man walked back into a puddle of liquid. As he stood there it gradually disappeared; it was obvious he had stood in the doorway to relieve himself.

'Dirty bastard,' muttered Roisin, 'No wonder it always stinks of piss in a morning.'

The tape ran further back.

'Stop! Play it from here forwards.'

Roisin did. They had a minute to wait because the tape had ticked back too far. But then there he was; Richard, walking past the shop. The time stamp read 00:14. Just after midnight.

Roisin had put on her reading glasses which showed how seriously she was taking this; she hated wearing them.

'Who's that with him?' she said.

Richard was not alone. There was a man alongside him, his face slanted towards him as if in conversation. He was shorter than Richard and much more lightly built. The image was monochrome but the man's hair looked light coloured.

'I don't know,' said Aidan, which, strictly was true. He did not know his name. He had seen him before though.

And the sight of him chilled him.

There was no doubt now. It was all connected.

It all led back to him.

It was the man who had turned up at the accident scene.

41

Chapter Seven

May 5th 1997 10.40pm

Roisin brought through two glasses and an opened bottle of white wine and put it on the table. She poured two large glasses and gave one to Aidan.

'Sorry, it's all I've got in,' she said.

'It's fine.'

'I think you need something stronger. You look terrified. You know something, don't you?'

Aidan didn't reply.

'So who is he? The man with Richard?'

'I told you, I don't know.'

'But you've seen him before?'

Aidan hesitated.

'Yes,' he said at last.

'Where? Come on Aidan, it's bloody obvious you know something. What is it?'

Aidan took a deep breath.

'Sod it,' he said. 'You might as well know.'

After he had finished Roisin puffed out her cheeks and shook her head.

'God, what a bloody idiot you are, Aidan Hughes. Driving pissed? I thought you knew better.'

'I was fine.'

'Of course you were. That's why there was an accident. That's why someone died.'

'But it wasn't my fault…'

'You were involved. And then you got poor Richard involved

and it killed him.'

Aidan reeled under this verbal assault.

'That's not fair. It was the Bentley driver that caused the accident and Richard wanted to be involved.'

'Yeah, you keep telling yourself that.' Roisin took a sip of her wine. 'You need to go to the police.'

He shook his head. 'I can't. Not now.'

'Why not now? Actually, I know; it's because you're a fucking coward, aren't you?' Roisin put her glass down. 'A coward who lets his friends down. To think I once thought you and me were...' Her voice trailed away, he could see that she was as angry with herself as with him.

Suddenly all his anger and tiredness, grief and frustration that had built up over the last few hours couldn't be kept inside him any more.

'What's the point of me going to the police now? What is the bloody point? Go on, tell me. Yes, Richard wasn't alone when he went to the City Tower but he was when he jumped, the police said that. So he met someone? Someone who was at the accident. So what? He didn't kill Richard, did he? Richard did that himself. We'll probably never know why but that's all there is to it.'

'But...'

'But nothing. There's nothing in this. Richard's dead. If I went and told them that wouldn't change but I'd be in trouble. I'd probably get prosecuted. I'd lose my job. I know you don't like me-'

'You're not wrong there,' muttered Roisin .

'Don't worry, you've made that quite obvious. Yeah, I'd pay for what I did, for driving off, but it wouldn't make any difference. It won't bring back the guy who died in the crash.' He sighed. 'And it won't bring Richard back, will it?'

Roisin 's head dropped. 'No.' She looked at her watch. 'Christ it's late,' she said. 'I've got to go to bed, I've got the shop to open up first thing.' She got to her feet. 'I should chuck you out, you deserve it, but I'm better than that. You can sleep on the sofa if you like.'

'Thanks.'

Roisin paused at the door. For a moment Aidan wondered if she'd changed her mind and was going to invite him to bed.

He was wrong.

'There's one thing you've forgotten,' she said. 'The passenger. The girl that survived the crash. If she remembers what happened then you'll be in the shit. That stupid car of yours isn't exactly common.' She smiled. 'And that'll make it worse for you with the cops if you haven't been to them first, won't it? Sleep well, Aidan.'

Chapter Eight

Aidan ordered a large coffee and a Danish and retreated to the farthest corner of the cafe, needing the double hit of sugar and black coffee to get going.

He hadn't slept well. Of course he hadn't, that was just what Roisin had intended.

She was right though; whether the girl remembered anything was crucial. And his car was memorable. That damned Alfa was more trouble than it was worth. He'd thought it would be good for his sex life but it had been towed more often than he'd pulled. He'd sell it, get something sensible and boring.

But that didn't solve his problem here and now.

There was a copy of the early edition of the paper on the next table that another customer had left. Aidan reached over and grabbed it before anyone else could. He flicked through it until he found what he was looking for.

The report was tucked away on page seven headlined 'Baby plucked from horror smash', followed by 'Tragic dad dies'. He had always questioned these sensationalised articles; everything was a horror, everyone who died was 'tragic' or something similar but this time Aidan actually knew the facts and knew it probably actually toned things down. Anyway, the basic facts were in the three paragraph story.

It did give the name of the car driver; Tomasz Bzryneski, and the fact that his wife and baby girl had been taken to Salford Hope Hospital, and that their injuries were not believed to be life-threatening.

But that was it. Nothing else. No mention of any other driver being involved. And the facts differed from what Aidan knew to be true; the reporter, apparently quoting a police spokesman, wrote that their car had crashed into a parked car and that police were still waiting to interview the passenger.

Aidan shook his head in disbelief; how could they have thought that? The facts just didn't fit – surely the analysis afterwards would show that? And the evidence of the eye witnesses.

Eyewitnesses?

There was just Aidan as far as he knew. Him and Mrs Bzryneski.

He needed to talk to her, to find out what she knew. Whether she recognised him. Whether she could help him get a start on the story.

But to do that he needed to find out more about her.

Which meant making a call he didn't want to make.

* * *

May 6th 1997 8.35am

He was conscious that he was still in yesterday's clothes as he sat down at his desk, not having had time to go back to his flat knowing that he couldn't be late again. Ah well, needs must.

As he needed to make this call.

It was with considerable trepidation that he punched the number into the phone.

'Suzie Regan.'

Even in her saying her name as she answered the phone he got a picture of what she would be like; busy, fizzing with energy, impatient.

'Hello Suzie, It's Aidan. Aidan Hughes. How are you?'

'How do you think I am? Rushed off my feet as usual. Deadlines pressing.'

He raised his eyebrows in exasperation as he looked at his watch. She did have a point; he should have waited until the afternoon when things eased down a little bit. Well, it was too late now.

'Yes, I'm sorry to bother you. It's about that fatal RTA in Matthew's Street on election night.'

'Yes, I remember. What about it?'

He had rehearsed what to say.

'I passed the crash scene a few minutes after it happened. I thought I recognised one of the cars involved. Do you have the names and backgrounds on the people in them?'

There was the briefest of pauses at the other end of the line.

'Aidan, I don't know what it's like on the business desk but we're pretty stretched here. We haven't the time to go checking on your mates.'

'Sorry, I wouldn't normally ask but…'

But what, he asked himself. What would he say if she really pushed it?

There was a sigh and the sound of some keyboard clicks from the other end of the line.

'They were Poles weren't they?' Suzie was more muttering to herself than talking to Aidan. 'Yes. Thomas and Rachel Bzryneski. Both technicians, one at Manchester Met, one at Salford Uni. Home address; Flat six, 31 Eden Court, Salford. That any help to you?'

'Er, yes, thanks.'

'Is it someone you know?'

'No. No, I didn't know them.'

'Right, well I'm so glad I was able to put your mind at rest.'

There was no sincerity in Suzie's voice. 'Wait a minute. Didn't Richard call me about this a couple of days ago? The morning before… well you know.'

'Did he? Oh right, I didn't know.'

'Crap. You must have, you practically sat on each other's laps.

What's going on?' Aidan felt like he had a bulldog attached to his trouser leg and that he was going to struggle to shake off.

'No, I didn't know, and, in case you've forgotten, Richard was my friend and it's been a bloody awful week here.'

He felt guilty that he had said it, and more guilty when there was an obviously pregnant pause before she replied. Silently, he apologised to Richard for using his death as cover.

'Oh, yes, right, sorry of course.' Susie was now full of bluster and clearly quite embarrassed. 'Poor Richard. It's terrible. I don't understand why and how he got so desperate that he would do such a thing. He's the last person who I thought would ever commit suicide.'

Her tone had entirely changed, the strident edge to her voice gone. There was clear affection. But Richard and Susie? Then again Richard was nothing if not unpredictable and could also be extremely charming.

'You're not the first person to say that to me in the last couple of days,' he said.

'You think that someone else was involved? Is it something to do with this accident? Was it Richard driving?'

Shit she was quick.

'No, he wasn't. There's no connection. It's just a coincidence.'

'I don't believe in coincidences.'

'Then you've got a nasty suspicious mind,' he said, attempting to laugh off her attention.

'That usually works for me. Look, Aidan, I can help if there's digging to do.'

He knew what that was; an unspoken suggestion that he wasn't up to this.

She was probably right.

'Look, there isn't. You're reading something into this that just isn't there.'

There was a pause on the other end of the line. You could almost feel Susie's frustration, could tell that she was weighing up what to do next. But before she did, he saw the chance to bring the call to an end..

'Well I've got to be...' he began but was interrupted mid-flow.

'Fancy going for a drink after work tonight?' she said.

He was completely taken aback. 'Er...well.'

'I want some grown-up company. Half the staff here are just kids straight out of uni and the rest just talk about babies, school places and league tables. Come on Aidan, take pity on me.'

'Well, yes, sure. That would be fun.'

He hoped that the insincerity in his words would come over and she'd back down on the offer.

She didn't.

'Great. About 6:30?'

'Yeah, fine.'

'See you then, bye.'

She put the phone down, leaving Aidan holding his handset and feeling rather stunned. What the hell just happened there? Suzie? Wanting to go out with him? That didn't seem right.

But he had what he needed to know.

* * *

May 6th 1997 10.20am

The half-truth he told the office was that he was going to interview the MD of a packaging company in Trafford Park that had just announced expansion plans. He was going there but not before visiting the hospital.

Parking the pool car on a nearby street, he made his way to the reception desk. He was not going to use his credentials to get in; they wouldn't have worked anyway.

'Hi. I wonder if you can help me, I'm looking for a friend of mine, well, a colleague actually. I've been away and just got back to find she's been in a terrible accident.'

Steady, he told himself, or you'll be in for a Bafta. The lady behind the desk was matronly with a pleasant disposition and keen to help.

'Well let's see what we can do,' she said turning to her computer. 'Now then my lovely what's your friend's name?'

'Rachel. Rachel Bzryneski. I work with her at the university.'

'Oh yes, she was in the paper. Lost a husband, that poor lamb.'

'Yes. That's right.'

'Well, she's in ward three. That's a general ward with open visiting so you should be in luck. Just follow the signs, you can't miss it.'

Aidan flashed her a relieved smile of thanks, which was genuine, but his heart was thumping. He paused by the Friend's shop, wondering whether he should buy some flowers but decided against it. He would go with no pretence.

He recognised her instantly despite the fact that he had only seen her fleetingly in the lights of the Bentley in the horrific moment before the crash. The image of her trapped in the car was burned indelibly into his memory too but an oxygen mask had obscured much of her face.

Her eyes closed, her head slightly turned, her blonde hair brushed back from her face, pale and drawn. She resembled a fragile, porcelain doll.

She opened her eyes and looked straight at him. There was no way that he could pretend he wasn't looking for her.

'Hello,' he said.

'Who are you?' she said.

Thank God he thought, she doesn't recognise me. That was all he needed to know. He should go.

Instead he found himself impelled to speak.

'I... I... saw the accident.'

He hadn't meant to say anything but, once said, he couldn't take it back; now he was committed.

She frowned, 'You did?' Her voice was weak, washed out, but

emotional and angry. 'They say Tomasz was at fault, which he drove into a stopped car. That is wrong. Tomasz was too careful.'

Glancing around him, Aidan realised that no one was looking at them. There was a chair by the pillow end of the bed, obviously placed there for visitors. Deciding to be bold, he pulled it over and sat down. He leaned close so he could speak to her without being overheard.

'He didn't,' he said in a low voice. 'The car he ran into was moving. It was on the wrong side of the road.'

Rachel's eyes opened wide. Then she turned her face away. Was that recognition?

'I kept saying to the police: Tomasz wouldn't do that. I told them I saw a car coming towards us. Two cars. One racing the other. They would not believe me.'

'That's what I saw.'

'They think I am crazy Polish woman. That I do not remember right. But I do remember.'

She started to cough, and clearly couldn't stop. Aidan realised it was hurting.

'There's water out in the corridor,' said the woman in the next bed. 'Don't just sit there. Go get her a drink.'

'Right, yes of course,' said Aidan, getting to his feet.

'It's taken you long enough to get in to see her,' said the woman.

'Sorry?'

'Leaving the poor thing alone all this time.'

'But I'm not...'

'Go get some water and stop making excuses. Girl's in pain. She's got broken ribs you know.' The voice was accusing.

Smarting with indignation, Aidan went into the corridor. The woman obviously assumed that Aidan was a boyfriend or a relative who had neglected her. Still it was good that Rachel backed up what he'd seen, he was beginning to doubt his own memory. Yet it deepened the mystery of why the police did not believe her. What sort of influence did the other driver have?

He found the water fountain alright, the standard type with the blueish plastic water bottle in the top. There was water in it but no cups. He stared at it, not knowing what to do.

'There's another on the next floor down,' said a passing nurse.

'Thanks.'

There was a staircase next to the machine, he went down and found a similar machine with three cups left in it. At first he filled one with water then realised he was being stupid and he'd be far better getting water from one upstairs so drained this one, giving himself a headache from the ice-cold liquid and, screwing his face up, headed back upstairs.

There was now an elderly woman in front of the water fountain, peering at it intently. She reached out and tentatively tried the water tap. She turned round and frowned at Aidan.

'I'm trying to get a drink for Betty,' she said.

'Betty?'

'Yes. She's in the ward there. Terrible dry she is, terrible. I can't find any cups.'

She looked pointedly at the ones in Aidan's hands.

'There are some downstairs,' he said then, seeing her face, gave in. 'But you can have one of these.'

She took one. 'Thank you, young man. Now how does this work?' she turned back to the water fountain, the cup in her hand.

'Here let me,' he said filling one cup and handing it to her.

'I want one, too,' said the lady, looking at the other cup.

'But...' began Aidan then bowed to the inevitability and filled the second one too. 'There you go,' he said but found that the old lady was already halfway back to the ward. Muttering some impolite words to himself, he followed, cup in hand.

'Sorry I was so long, Betty,' said the woman, 'I had a few problems but this kind young man came to my rescue.'

Betty looked at Aidan and smiled. 'That's all right, Doris. Well, you're a fine young chap. What's your name?'

'Aidan.'

A banal conversation began to which Aidan contributed to in desultory, disinterested fashion. He just wanted to get away. He didn't want to appear too rude. All the time his eyes were fixed on the bed at the top end of the ward. He could see that there was now a doctor with Rachel. He was glad he'd been away from the bed when he'd arrived. Another man stood a little way back, a relative perhaps? If so, he'd been doubly lucky.

'So are you married, young man?' said Doris.

'No'

'Fine looking lad like you? What a waste. Are you courting?' said Betty.

It was like being transported back to visits he had as a child to a pair of maiden aunts, dragged there by his mother.

'No... not as such.'

'You're one of those 'omosexuals are you?' said Doris.

'No!' said Aidan, rather more loudly than he intended. A number of people in the beds turned around and look towards him. 'No,' he added more quietly.

'He's just playing the field,' said Betty.

'Well, we won't keep you,' said Doris. They had had their fun and were quite content to let him go now.

He hesitated, not quite sure what to do. He didn't want to go back to Rachel's bedside whilst a doctor was there but there wasn't really anywhere else to go. The doctor was clearly telling Rachel something confidential, he was leaning right up to her and she seemed to be concentrating hard, her eyes fixed on his face. He remembered that he still had no water for Rachel so went on a new mission to get a cup. This took longer than expected as the sole cup he had left in the downstairs one had gone and he had to go hunting on other floors. When he returned he was pleased to see that Rachel was alone.

That was odd, he'd expected that the other man, the 'relative', would have stayed.

'There you are,' he said, putting the cup on her bedside. Rachel looked surprised. There was no recognition on her face.

'Hello,' she said, 'Do I know you?'

'Yes. We talked before the doctor came.'

'Doctor?'

This was turning into a farce. He half expected someone was going to jump out and shout April fool at any moment.

'Never mind. You were telling me before about the accident, about what you remember?'

'Yes,' she said, 'Tomasz crashed into parked car. I screamed warning. I don't understand why he didn't see it.'

Aidan just stared at her.

Chapter Nine

Aidan's head was still reeling when he got back to the office. He had gone through the meeting in Trafford Park on autopilot. He realised halfway through that the man seemed to be irritated and Aidan couldn't, at first, see the reason for this until he realised that he himself was the problem; disinterested and detached, he was coming over as being extremely rude.

He was still distracted when writing up the story, which meant it took longer than it should have. Why had Rachel Bzryneski changed her story? Was it the effects of the accident? Did she have a brain injury? No, he decided, if she did she wouldn't have been in a general ward. So what else could explain it?

Only one thing; someone had got to her. But the only person who'd spoken to her was the doctor and…

'Oh you bloody idiot!' he muttered to himself.

He'd only assumed it was a doctor. It was him, the blond man, popping up where there was chaos and death. The other one had to be his minder. Aidan had thought he'd looked familiar.

What could you say to a grieving widow to change a story? To the police to release the road rage driver? Rachel Bzryneski, a foreigner, certainly, but Polish, an EU member, free labour movement and all that, no question of immigration problems, the same for a late husband. Was it a threat then? A physical threat? It was possible, but she didn't seem frightened, not even shocked and confused.

Not a threat then.

Whatever it was, another avenue had closed. The story, Richard's story, was as far away as ever.

But Richard had got close and had died for it; how?

It had started with one lead, that company name, the one he'd got from Carole, the one with the access to the police database. What was it? Richard had written it on a post-it note. Aidan spotted it on the side of Richard's in-tray.

Written in Richard's familiar, untidy handwriting was the name: Astcanza.

A company name. That was better. It gave him somewhere to start. Aidan turned to his computer and opened the newly launched Company's House website.

A few minutes later he sat back, disappointed at how little he'd found out. Astcanza was a private company. Two directors were listed, both doctors; Mitchell Finch and Gerhard Beck, and that it worked in the Biotech field. That was it. Nothing else. Private companies did not have to file details like a PLC. Dead end.

Well maybe not completely. He opened Netscape and did a search, hoping to find out more. There wasn't much. There were Astcanzas in other countries, but only one mention from Britain, a press release announcing its launch, the typical thing that Aidan had written for a hundred other businesses. It was the right one, Doctors Finch and Beck were the directors, the company set up to exploit opportunities generated from the men's academic work.

But it said nothing about what these opportunities were.

Frustrating.

He did a search on Dr Mitchell Finch and Dr Gerhard Beck. Little, if any, related to a business. Most of the hits he found for Beck found seem to be connected with the man's academic work and, judging by the language, most of his work had been in Germany. Aidan struggled to understand any of the titles, let alone work out what they were about, though he thought he recognised the word genetics in the text.

Mitchell Finch also had some academic papers but in an entirely different field: business, in magazines like Forbes and Investors Chronicle. There were also links to his departmental homepage at UMIST. Searching again, this time for images, produced photographs of both men. Beck was short, dark and plump and somehow distinctly Eastern European whilst Finch was tall and angular, staring superciliously down his nose at the camera in each shot. Neither man was the psychopathic driver or the blond man.

So a dead end, or perhaps at best a lead that was not relevant?

* * *

He was disappointed; this was one area where he really thought he could get somewhere. Every door was being slammed in his face.

Richard had got somewhere.

Richard was a better reporter. He never gave up. Aidan had lost his mentor but he could at least follow his lead.

He did Company's House searches of the other directorships for the two men. Beck had nothing but Mitchell Finch had two other recorded directorships. One was a recruitment company; that fitted in with his academic work. The other company Aidan was sure he recognised; Urbania.

Urbania Limited. He checked its registered address and found, to no surprise, that it was in Sale, Cheshire, on a business park. Another private company though.

There were three other directors listed as well as Finch: Rashid Ahmed, Peter Smith and Michael Smith.

Aidan frowned. Ahmed and Smith. Common names. Searching for their surnames wouldn't get him anywhere. Typical.

The company though, that was different. Urbania. One of those irritating corporate names so beloved by branding experts. Aidan ran another search on the name Smith against the company name.

It produced results and more of the jigsaw slotted into place. Now he remembered. Urbania was a property development company. It burst onto the scene apparently from nowhere about four years ago with a controversial scheme in the Northern quarter.

Maxwell Mill.

It had become a cause célèbre for the conservation movement. A listed building, Grade II*, part of the industrial heritage of Manchester, the best part of 200 years old and still in use, not as a textile mill but a nursery for over a hundred small firms. The problem was it was located slap bang in one of the most fashionable parts of an increasingly fashionable city. Its location made it an obvious target for developers. The new Manchester was rising as a model post-industrial city, just as it had blazed the trail for the Industrial Revolution.

Maxwell Mill had stood against the trend, against the 20th tide of renaissance that swept through the city. Certainly developers had always had it in their sights, but if Aidan's memory was right, it was too difficult to develop, there were too many tenants with too strong or long leases that couldn't be ended or bought out; too many conservation groups had expressed interest and concerns for a development to succeed.

Many developers had tried and failed, bailing out through bankruptcy or huge losses.

But then Urbania came on the scene. The company no one had heard of, with no track record. Aidan had a niggling memory of them getting consents easily for the scheme and also got the council to use the compulsory purchase powers to clear the building within a few months. This all brought howls of protest from the small businesses, the interest groups and even within the council itself.

But still it had succeeded.

He called up the newspaper records on Urbania.

What they revealed was a company active in the property market but having a remarkably low profile. They were almost publicity shy, very unusual in the sector; most developers trumpeted their schemes way before they'd even broken ground. Not Urbania. It was not until they'd got consent or actually started building had they announced their ownership. The other schemes they were involved with were difficult ones, ones that the other developers had tried and failed with, ones that would be problems, the ones that would be difficult to fund. It never seemed to have problems in this front either; it always seemed to get development loans from a variety of sources, even through the storms in the financial markets, Urbania came through. They seemed to defy gravity.

Aidan went back to his musing. He thought back to a seminar he was sent to on development when he was trying to get a handle on property after his transfer to the business pages. His editor tried to improve his knowledge and had sent him on a few appropriate professional courses. The one on development had stuck, perhaps because the presenter had charisma and had delivered the material in a really accessible and quite entertaining manner. He made it clear that firstly, development had huge potential risk because of the combination of the geared relationship of end value to input costs and the very long timescales involved in projects that made the return potentially much higher than most other fields. In particular, if you could buy cheap and solve the problems on a difficult site, then the rewards could be absolutely enormous. The problem was that risk could be magnified, potential losses too, if things went wrong, enough to send most developers into receivership.

Yet that seemed to be precisely what Urbania's business model was. Take on the difficult projects. Take on the risk. Maximise the return.

Aidan sat back. This was all very interesting, but where was the link to the accident? He needed to find one.

Once again he did a search, this time on the people involved. Mitchell Finch appeared on a few photographs, mainly at launch parties of completed developments; he looked ill at ease in them. The suits had certainly improved from his academic days but his face was thinner and his eyes had a haunted quality about them. That was not a happy man, that was someone under strain. Rashid Ahmed was on one of the photographs as well, captioned as the company's director of finance. There were also some photographs of Peter Smith but none of his brother Michael. One article he found was longer and mentioned the brothers background; scrap metal and waste management.

Weird.

Aidan couldn't believe it. The Smiths were scrappers before starting Urbania?

Scrap metal? Another dead end. Not businesses to keep many records at all, certainly none that would be reported online.

He looked at photographs of Peter Smith. He wasn't the

driver either but his look and build were similar; thick neck, huge shoulders, shaved head, someone who spent years in a combination of heavy manual labour and the gym, with some steroid abuse thrown in.

So was the driver his brother Michael? From the looks he could be.

The one long article on Urbania, written four years before, at about the time Urbania emerged with the Maxwell Mill scheme, was by someone clearly trying to get to the bottom of the company. They must have failed because there didn't seem to be any follow-up articles on the Smith brothers. It was the article itself that hinted at some mystery about them, including rumours that the brothers were like chalk and cheese. Peter the muscle, the brawn, the other - Michael, or Mickey - although younger, was the leader, the brains, the thinker, the strategist. He was the one taking them from the murky world on the edge of legality in the hard graft of scrap metal to respectability, to the nouveau rich of the Manchester business world.

Mickey Smith was reclusive though, he kept out of sight letting others take the limelight. The article concluded that, for all the talk was that this man was the driving force behind Urbania, no one had asked the key question; who was he really?

Aidan wondered who had authored the article. It would be useful to talk to him. He flicked to the top.

'Bloody hell,' he said, loudly enough for others around to look at him.

The article was by Richard Tasker.

Chapter Ten

May 6th 1997 7.05pm

It was late when Aiden got back to his desk thanks to one of Gill's editorial meetings.

The meeting - planning the paper's in-depth response to 'Manchester under New Labour' - were the longest hours of his life. He had spent most of it daydreaming and doodling, almost drifting off to sleep at one point. Gill had, of course, chosen that moment to ask him a direct question, and he was fuming and frustrated by the time it was finally over. At last he could get back to Urbania.

The office was looking distinctly deserted by the time he got back. He was surprised to find there was someone sat at his desk.

It was Suzie Regan.

'Hi Suzie,' he said.

His voice made her jump.

'Ah, at last,' she said, sitting up. She had been bent over his keyboard, looking at the display. His eyes went straight to it. What had he left on there? She'd minimised the screen. Had she been snooping? 'Long meeting?' she said.

'Yeah, editorial planning. Been in it since four.'

'A marathon,' she said. 'You must be frazzled.'

Aidan had to hand it to her; If she had been looking she didn't look the slightest bit guilty.

'A bit,' he said. He nodded at his chair. 'Do you mind? I need to check my emails.'

'Of course,' she said, getting up to let him sit. As he passed her he got a heady nose full of her scent; she had clearly recently refreshed it. He was no expert but was pretty certain it was Chanel; expensive anyway. It lingered on his chair which was still warm from her body. It was all quite an assault on his senses.

'I was checking the weather.' she said. 'We're having a barbecue next weekend.'

At least she felt the need to make an excuse.

'No problem,' he said. He glanced across; why wasn't she leaving? 'So what do I owe the pleasure of this visit?'

'Really? We were going for a drink, remember? I left you a voicemail.'

'Did you? I've had my phone off. Oh yeah, the drink. That was now?'

'That's what we arranged. That's all right isn't it?'

'Yes of course. Sorry, the evening's sort of galloped up on me all of a sudden. And,' he added, 'it's been a very long week. With Richard and everything.'

Her face fell.

'Yes. Poor Richard. But he's all the more reason to get out of this place. He wouldn't want us moping around. Let's you and me go and have enough to drink to make life feel more pleasant. You on for it?'

As Aidan had just found that the sum total of his importance in the two and three quarter hours he had spent in the meeting was summed up in the grand total of five emails, three of which were junk, he couldn't really argue with her, even if he did really want to do more digging into Urbania and the Smith brothers.

'Sure,' he said. 'That sounds like a bloody good idea.'

* * *

May 6th 1997 8.05pm

Aidan was in a slide into alcohol induced haze. It was a path well-trodden.

But the company was much less familiar; Suzie. As he expected it was she who dominated the conversation but she stayed away from their late friend until they were well into their third round.

'It must be odd without him,' she said, her face suddenly serious.

'It's weird. I keep expecting him to just wander in looking like he always did. It'll take a while to sink in.'

Suzie nodded. Her eyes were fixed on her drink, deep in contemplation allowing Aidan to look at Suzie more closely, something he'd not really dared do before. She was good-looking; handsome if not classically pretty with a big eyes and dark, gypsy curls. But he noticed something that surprised him; her nails were filed right down, unvarnished, and redness about the nail beds suggested that she bit them. That was not a common habit in a woman, and unexpected in her. It suggested someone who lived on her nerves, behind a facade.

'I'm not looking forward to the funeral,' she muttered. 'I really don't fancy meeting Alison again.'

Alison was Richard's ex-wife, the last of three exes in fact.

Interesting. Maybe those rumours were right.

'Do you really think he committed suicide?' she said abruptly.

The question, though obvious, put him in a spot. He hesitated before saying 'Yes.'

The hesitation was enough to give himself away.

'Liar,' she said. It was a statement rather than rather an accusation. 'So what has Urbania to do with it?'

So she had been looking at his browsing history.

'Snooping isn't nice,' he said angrily, though whether this was with Suzie or himself for being careless and leaving the pages up for all to see on his PC, he wasn't quite sure. 'And nothing, that was about something else.'

'Oh yeah, pull the other one. I don't believe you.'

'So what if you don't?'

'So what? What the hell do you think you're doing? You're not an investigative reporter. You're totally out of your depth.'

'Cheers. Thank you so very much. Thanks for the drink, thanks for the evening. Now sod off.'

But it was Aidan who was on his feet and heading to the door whilst his words still bounced off the walls. He was conscious of eyes on him; everyone would probably think this was a lover's tiff and he was walking out in a huff. Well he didn't care what they thought, he just wanted to get away. Out on the street he headed off towards the square and the tram stop.

There was a clatter of heels behind him.

'Aidan! Aidan! Come on, this is silly. Don't make me chase you. Not in these shoes.'

He ignored her and kept walking.

'Please Aidan, I'm sorry. I didn't mean what I said. Please!'

He stopped. He actually needed to; he was out of breath. He couldn't believe how out of shape he was.

'I am sorry. Honest.'

'Okay', he said. 'Thanks,' and started walking again. He heard her follow.

'Where are you going?' she said.

'Home,' he said.

'Okay,' she said. 'But we need to talk about Urbania.'

'There's nothing to talk about.'

They had reached the tram stop. The digital display indicated that the next one was due in nine minutes. That was a long time to wait. Damn. It gave Suzie a chance to get at him.

She took it.

'Yes there is, I just know that there is. You wouldn't have had it on your computer if there wasn't a connection.'

'Of course I would. I'm a business correspondent, remember?' he said. 'Companies are my remit.'

'Not companies like Urbania.'

'Yes like them. They're developers. Property, that's my field, yes?'

'You know what I mean. You know that there are questions about them?'

'What questions?'

'Questions that Richard investigated. You saw the article.'

'Yes, but that was a one off.' As soon as he uttered the words he realised his mistake; Richard was not one to stop once his curiosity had been roused. It wouldn't have been a one-off. 'Wasn't it?' he added.

'No, it wasn't. He went deeper. He had massive suspicions about them, he was sure they were really dirty, a front for organised crime, but couldn't make anything stick.'

Aidan was stunned. 'I didn't know that,' he said quietly. 'But how do you-'

'I was working with him at the time, a cub reporter shadowing him.'

'Oh, right.'

'You know what he was like, sometimes he could smell a story. He knew there was one and it frustrated him that he couldn't get anywhere. He thought that they were laughing at him. He said that they were scary people, that Urbania was the public face, the legitimate business that gave them an acceptable façade to the outside world, but underneath they were rotten to the core.'

'They wouldn't be the first or the only one,' said Aidan.

'Exactly.'

'But it still doesn't mean that either of us were investigating them this time.'

'Oh come on, Aidan, who are you trying to kid?'

Aidan said nothing. He stared at the red numbers of the display; still three minutes to go before the next tram.

'Look,' she said, 'I'm not going to forget this. I'm not going to give up. I'm going to start digging into Urbania now with or without your help.'

'Good luck to you.'

'Come on, I'm a far better investigative reporter than you are. Wouldn't you rather have me on your side rather working against you?'

She looked earnest. What to do? He didn't want to bring another person into the story. Yes, it was weird, potentially dangerous but this still might be his golden ticket.

Yet she was right, she was better than he was. Richard had said she was the brightest cookie he had seen, that she was brazen and tenacious, qualities that Aidan was not famous for. Perhaps he would be better with her. He almost said yes but then the tram redeemed itself by arriving.

'Night,' he said getting to his feet. 'Maybe see you tomorrow.'

He was pleased to see her look surprised, disappointed, deflated and frustrated in quick succession.

'I thought you were brighter than this,' she said. 'But you're just another pig-headed male, aren't you?'

'Sorry to be a disappointment,' he said, stepping into the tram. 'You're not the first woman to tell me that.'

She stepped up after him, fumbling with a pen and a business card.

'This is my private number and address. If you come to your senses, call me.'

The buzzer sounded, warning that the doors were about to close. Suzie barely made it back onto the tram platform.

On the journey he wondered over and over whether he had just done the right thing.

The jury on that one was still out as he walked up the road towards his flat.

When he got to the car park he stopped and stared at the space where his car normally stood. Where was it?

Then he remembered.

'Shit,' he muttered.

It was in for its repairs and MOT. He'd meant to check with

the garage to see if it was done, it was supposed to be today "without fail, squire". Actually they'd said they'd ring when it was finished and obviously hadn't. Damn and blast them. And damn and blast Suzie Regan. If she hadn't dragged him out for that pointless drink then he'd have remembered. Now he would have to sort things out tomorrow. He could do without that.

Still in a black mood he let himself into the block's front door and trudged up the stairs. His next flat, he told himself, would be on the ground floor.

When he got his landing he saw his front door was ajar. He swore and stepped inside. His worst fears were realised; his flat had been trashed.

Now, having avoided them for days, he called the police.

Chapter Eleven

May 6th 1997 10.15pm

It was the best part of two hours later that Aidan got rid of them. He wasn't impressed.

A patrol had been nearby and two officers arrived within fifteen minutes of his call. They offered a degree of sympathy, some comments on the inadequacy of the lock on his front door and his lack of a burglar alarm and a took a statement. He was also asked to make a list of anything that was missing, which seemed to amount to his DVD player.

That was it.

'We don't normally attend burglaries on nights,' one said. 'But we were close so thought we might catch the scroats in the act. Little sods look long gone though.'

'Looks like you were lucky, Mr Hughes,' said the other. 'They were looking for cash or stuff they could turn quickly and didn't find them. You've got a hell of a mess but you haven't lost much. You find anything else has gone just give the station a call, quoting the incident number we gave you.'

'Yes, will do. Thanks.'

Thanks for nothing, Aidan thought.

He started to tidy up but he was distracted by hunger pangs. He'd not eaten anything since a BLT at lunchtime. He considered finishing the tidying first but saw the time, the takeaway would be closing soon too. Better go now.

He paused at the door. Something bothered him about it. He had a Yale latch and a mortice lock. Neither looked like they'd been forced. He'd been burgled before and that hadn't been at all subtle; then his door had been prised open, wrecking it. This time his door was unmarked, he assumed he'd left it on the Yale and that had been sprung with a flexible blade. That was what the police had assumed as well, chiding him for his forgetfulness in not double-locking it.

But that didn't make sense either. He'd tried to break into a room with a Yale lock once when he'd locked himself out and found that it was nowhere near as easy as suggested on TV. He'd done a lot of damage as he struggled to get the blade in the right place. This was different, it was neat, hardly a sign left that anyone had interfered with the lock. He was also not convinced that he hadn't double locked the door; he rarely forgot. In fact, the more he thought about it he could not remember the last time that he'd forgotten.

With this in mind, Aidan looked around the devastated flat with fresh eyes. Now, rather than looking like an inept job where the thieves had made a lot of mess but taken very little, a nuisance rather than a major blow, it looked much more like a professional search lightly disguised to look like a normal break-in.

So what were they looking for? There was one connection that was obvious; a rat that was smelling very strongly indeed.

In somewhat of a daze Aidan shut and double locked the flat door, wondering if it was a futile exercise, and headed to the takeaway. He tried to think rationally but it was difficult to get beyond his fear.

What did he have to worry about? They wouldn't have found anything because there was nothing to find. Wouldn't that mean they would give up? If it was them in the first place – and, of course, he didn't really know who 'them' were. And anyway, they couldn't possibly have known who Aidan was, could they?

Well, yes, they could if they had Richard's phone. They would have known that Richard had called him that night, the night that Richard died. But how had they traced him? It was only a mobile number. Actually it wouldn't have been that hard, he realised; Aidan's phone was on contract. Contracts meant that his address was held by the mobile operator. Once that information was stored somewhere then it could be accessed, even if it was supposed to be private and secure. Where there was a corporate or a criminal need, a way could always be found. It might only take a few days and it had, of course, been a few days since Richard died.

So if they could do that, what else could they do?

By this time he had reached the Chinese. He was not sure that he was hungry now but decided to go through the motions. Rather than spend time choosing he chose the easy route and ordered the banquet for one again.

'Okay. Five minute. You wait,' said the Chinese girl behind the counter, scribbling down the order and thrusting it through the hatch behind a with the usual rapid burst of Chinese to which she received a completely unintelligible reply.

Aidan sat with another customer. A portable TV was playing on a high shelf behind the counter, greasily wedged between some garish red and gold plastic ornaments. The girl perched on a stool watching intently. Aidan was expecting it to be some music show but, no, the girl was clearly a science geek because the camera lingered on a familiar face to Aidan, Bryn Parry, as he explained some physics theory to the masses. Bloody hell, that was the last thing he needed tonight; a repeat of his old friend's vehicle to fame and fortune. It was difficult enough to stomach the first time round.

He turned and stared out into the night. Was the burglary a professional job? Really? Or was he just getting paranoid? Probably, he decided. He had had a very traumatic week; he was tired, spooked by the slightest thing.

Like the black BMW that had drawn up across the road from whom no one had got out. His mind found it could invent all sorts of menacing things, like that the driver and passenger were watching him.

In reality the people inside were probably doing something perfectly innocent.

Like drug dealing.

He smiled to herself. He really was losing it.

For something to do he called the voicemail service on his mobile. There was no message waiting sign so he didn't expect anything so it was no surprise then when the female voice said: 'You have no new messages.' After a pause she went on to say. 'You have... five... saved messages.'

'Five?' he said out loud making the girl at the counter and the other customer look at him.

He knew that he had a couple saved from business calls earlier week but where had the other ones come from?

The last and first of the new ones were calls from the garage, both occurring during the meeting that afternoon when his phone was turned off and when any incoming calls were automatically diverted to voicemail, sandwiching one from Suzie reminding Aidan about going for that drink.

He remembered that she'd said she'd called but he had assumed that was to the office phone. It was news to him that she had his mobile number. Whatever, as she said, it was just a reminder about going for the drink. The first call from the garage was to tell him his car was done, the second, slightly more irritated in tone, informed him they were shutting up shop at 5:30 and 'could you please come and get his car now?'

This was a puzzle. Why hadn't his phone notified him he'd got messages when he turned it on after the meeting? It always did, it'd never let him down before.

Unless... unless someone had read his texts and accessed his voicemail before he had.

Oh bloody hell, he thought, could his phone be hacked? He had heard it was possible but had no idea how it was done or who, outside MI5 and the police, could do it. Why would anyone bother? He was nothing, a nobody - except that he was a witness to a certain accident and that the aftermath to it may have cost his friend's life.

May have. Could have. Or he could just be paranoid.

On reflection that was much more likely.

'Banquet for one,' sang the girl, holding a cardboard carrier up to the room in general, even though they were still only two customers. Aidan went and claimed it.

As he left the takeaway he glanced across at the BMW. He could make out two figures in it, both men, but that was about it for details. He certainly couldn't see their faces.

Paranoid, he was definitely getting paranoid.

Aidan headed back to his flat, a walk that took him only five minutes. As he unlocked the front door he saw the black BMW draw up on the far side of the street.

He didn't enjoy his Chinese.

Chapter Twelve

May 7th 1997 8.45am

The first thing that Aidan did the next day was to go and retrieve his car, taking the hit on his wallet with a weak smile a renewed resolution to sell it and get something more sensible.

The second thing was to drive to a retail park and make a single purchase; the cheapest pay-as-you-go mobile phone he could find complete with five pounds worth of credit.

He sat in the car, hesitating to take the next step. There would be no going back once he'd taken it.

He had decided in the middle of a long, largely sleepless night that he needed help, that he couldn't do this alone.

It seemed obvious then, now he was not so sure. Was it the right thing? He'd throw away his chance to do something big on his own.

He'd to go it alone, the fears of the night driven away by the light of day. But then he noticed, in his rear view mirror, a black BMW with two men in it, parked two rows behind him in the half empty car park.

Now without hesitation (and without taking his eyes off a car in his mirror) he tapped in the number, trying to control his rapidly beating heart, trying to keep the fear out of his voice.

'Suzie? It's Aidan. No, it's not my normal phone. Can we meet up somewhere today, preferably in the office? No, I'd rather not say why now...'

* * *

May 7th 1997 9.50am

They met in one of the meeting rooms on the fourth floor. Suzie listened to Aidan without comment all the way through. What did that mean, that she didn't believe him?

'Well, that's it,' he said. Now he had told it to someone he began to doubt himself again. 'There's not much to go on, I know that. I really don't know if I'm just being paranoid.'

His voice trailed off, expecting a sceptical reply from Suzie.

It didn't come.

'No. I don't think you're being paranoid at all, there's something going on and it stinks to high heaven,' she said.

Aidan sighed with relief, a huge burden lifted from his shoulders.

'Do you think I should go to the police?'

Suzie looked astounded. 'Are you kidding? she said. 'This could be massive. Why should we give it all away?'

'I was just checking,' he said quickly. 'I don't trust my judgement lately.'

'Well, you've done okay so far.'

Aidan had a flash of anger at this condescension but then remembered this was Suzie who had a famously abrasive personality and a sometimes unfortunate turn of phrase. Richard had defended her more than once, saying her abrasiveness was inadvertent, that she rarely did it deliberately. It was just the way she was so he counted to ten.

'So what do we do now?' he said at last.

'We need to do more digging, see if we can get a firm link from Urbania to the accident and to Richard's death.'

'How?'

'We could do with digging out some photos of Mickey Smith, to see if you recognise him.'

Aidan nodded.

'Is it worth doing some digging into Urbania itself, the way they work?'

Suzie pulled a face.

'Better people than us have looked at them and got nowhere. Whatever they do they cover their tracks pretty well. I think it's a waste of time...but you can do it if you want, I guess.'

Aidan had another flash of annoyance but Suzie gave no sign of having noticed his irritation. She tapped her pen on the notes she had made.

'What's the connection with this Astcanza outfit? That seems an odd match-up. What are a couple of university lecturers doing tied up with the Smith brothers? You could do that while I dig into the latest stuff on the Smiths.'

'Will you have time?' said Aidan, rapidly seeing his story slipping away. 'What about the day job?'

'Don't worry about that. Phil knows better than to get in my way,' she waved a hand in airy dismissal. 'My stuff sells papers. I'll have a word on the QT. He'll make sure my work gets shunted off to someone else. Got a couple of grads; it's about time they pulled their weight.'

Phil was the news editor, Suzie's line manager. Aidan knew him only by reputation as a both a hard taskmaster and someone who had national ambitions – even though he was getting a bit long-in-the-tooth for it. He probably would let Suzie run with the story expecting it to go nowhere but would quickly step in to take a big share of the credit if they succeeded and claim no knowledge if it went wrong. This brought it home to him that his quiet, unobtrusive career path was over. He was out in the open now, playing for higher stakes.

'I'd really like to know why the police let him go. I've got a few contacts at GMP. I'll see what I can get.'

'Be careful,' said Aidan. 'Getting stuff from the police is a sensitive issue these days.'

Suzie gave him a withering stare.

'I wasn't born yesterday. I know what I'm doing,' she snapped.

'Sorry, yes, of course.'

There was an awkward silence for a few moments. Aidan broke it by saying; 'So what else should we look into?'

'As I said, the university connection is interesting. Where is Finch at?'

'UMIST. Or at least he was.'

'Was? He's left?'

'I don't know.'

'Strange place that.'

'What, UMIST?'

'Yeah, everyone I met from there when I was at the Met were all geeks, especially the girls. Less stuck up than the other lot though.'

Suzie had gone to Manchester Met and had been dismissive before when she'd found he'd done English at Manchester University itself – but that thought reminded him of something else; the face from the TV last night.

'I know someone who works UMIST,' he said. 'In fact, I shared a house with them.'

'I hardly think one of your uni pals is going to be any use to us.'

He ignored her dismissal because he knew he definitely had one over her this time.

'I think you might have heard of him...Bryn Parry? He fronted that big physics series that the BBC did last year.'

He was delighted to see her mouth drop open.

'Bryn Parry? Doctor Bryn? You know him?'

'Yes. Very well actually, though it's a couple of years since we last met up.'

'Why didn't you say before you knew him?'

'I didn't think it was all that much of a big deal. He's nothing special.'

'Nothing special? The thinking woman's crumpet? You knew him all this time and didn't tell anyone?'

Aidan shrugged. 'It never crossed my mind.'

'I'll come with you when you go to see him.'

'Yeah, well, I'll have to find out if he's free of course, I imagine he's pretty busy,' said Aidan, resolving to make certain he'd 'forget' to tell her when he went to see his old friend.

He had developed a certain blind spot with Bryn; he found his latest television appearances irritating. When he had first started to pop up on programmes, Aiden was pleased for his friend's success. It had come out of the blue; he had lost touch with Bryn a few years after university as their career paths had diverged. His recent fame had, if Aidan was being honest with himself, been like a punch in his stomach to him. As students, although on very different courses, there had not been very much to separate them. In fact, the only thing that Bryn had over Aidan was his easy charm; it made people like him instantly. It was just the same easy charm that he was now using to good effect in his media career. It had been a surprise that Bryn's degree was as good as it had been in the end, the result of cramming at the end of the year getting him well over the line and, instead of going to work in industry as was expected, he accepted a PhD scholarship.

'We ought to find out more about Mitchell Finch before we go and see him,' said Suzie, bringing Aidan back to the present. 'Can you do that, Aidan? I've already started on the Smiths.' She met Aidan's surprised look with a challenging one of her own. 'Well, what did you expect? That I was to go home like a good girl and forget what I'd seen you were looking at? There was no way I was ever going to do that.'

'I guess not,' conceded Aidan.

'Right then. I'll go and sort Phil out, keep him sweet then we'll get together later.'

'Today?'

'Yes, of course today. We don't want this story going stale do we? You can swing this with Gill, can't you? Or do you want me to have a word with her? We're good mates, you know. We're in the same hockey team.'

Aidan didn't know but, on reflection, he could have guessed; both women had the sleek frame and ruddy complexion of the outdoor sportswoman and he recalled seeing them leaving the office together carrying sports bags.

'No. I'll speak to her. No need for you to bother.' Aidan had actually decided to say nothing to Gill, not with her obvious suspicions about what he had known about Richard. 'You're not going to tell Phil the full details are you?'

'God, no, there's no need to do that. Phil will trust my instincts and take my word for it that it's important.' She looked at her watch. 'Let's meet together at, what, five?'

She got to her feet and flashed a brief smile at Aidan as she left the meeting room.

Aidan waited a few minutes, thinking. Suzie Regan. Bloody hell, she was worse than he'd thought.

'Well, you've done it now,' he muttered to himself.

With a weary sigh, he headed back to his desk.

Chapter Thirteen

Aiden didn't have a great deal of enthusiasm for his normal work but with a bit of effort and working over his lunch hour he finally got it done.

Then he went out to buy a late, slightly stale, sandwich and found somewhere to sit and think.

He wrote down names on a fresh page in his notebook: Richard, Mitchell Finch, Gerhard Beck, Mickey Smith (who he put a question mark against), the blond man - all around a single word; accident. How did they fit together?

The links between the nodes were tenuous. He also had the question mark against Mickey Smith; he had no proof that the man was even involved. As Suzie had said, he needed to see a picture of him. He looked at the names Mitchell Finch and Gerhard Beck. What were their connections with all this? How did two directors of another company, two academics, fit into this pattern? Maybe not at all. All he had was the second Bentley registered to their company.

Aidan gathered up the debris of his lunch and threw them in the bin. He felt satisfied even though his exercise had not produced any solid progress. It had, at least, focused his thinking, showing where it needed work. He was clearer about the issues. It would impress Suzie.

Impress her? Why did he feel he needed to? Did he need Suzie at all? It was too late now, that genie was well out of the bottle. She would have her uses, he was sure. She had contacts.

His eyes went back to the names of the two academics. Here

he had the contact, one that Suzie wanted to exploit. Sod her; he was not going to roll over and let her walk all over him.

Back at the office he hunted in his desk drawer for his old address book. He looked up Bryn Parry.

There were a series of addresses and crossed out telephone numbers that illustrated years of a footloose existence that Aidan himself had gone through at the same age. There were a number of work numbers for Bryn too, albeit less of them than Aidan himself had. The last one was a number at UMIST. Aidan couldn't remember the last time he had rung it, if, in fact, he ever had. It was years old. He pulled a face; typical, the one advantage he had over Suzie and the number was probably out of date.

Maybe if he called it he might get through to someone who could find Bryn's number on an internal directory? With very little hope he dialled.

'Good afternoon, Bryn Parry?'

The response came so quickly that momentarily Aidan was unable to think what to say.

'Hello?' said Bryn again.

'Bryn,' Aidan found his voice. 'It's Aidan Hughes. How are you?'

'Well hello stranger. How the devil are you?'

'Fine thanks. How about you?'

'Not too bad. Overworked and underpaid but that's academia for you.'

'I thought you were a television star now.'

There was a laugh from the other end of the line. 'Oh that. More trouble than it's worth, actually. It was fun though and it seemed to go down well. So what are you doing these days? Still at the paper?'

'Yes, still here.'

'We ought to get together for a drink,' said Bryn.

Aidan gave a silent fist pump.

'That's exactly why I called. I thought it was about time we caught up.'

'It is. Can you come over now?'

'Now?'

'Yeah, why not? I've not got anything in my diary.'

'Yes, then, no problem.'

Aidan was thinking of a problem, a Suzie shaped one. Despite what he'd decided, she'd said she wanted to come along. Well, tough, bringing along his abrasive new ally would be hard to explain to his old friend.

'Great. Do you know where you are coming to?' said Bryn.

He gave directions to his office, a building that Aidan remembered picking Bryn up from in his student days. It would be the first time he'd been back to it since he had left.

Aidan guessed that it would feel very odd indeed.

But it was still progress.

Chapter Fourteen

May 7th 1997 4.15pm

It did feel odd.

It also felt odd to be in his old friend's company. It was a sharp reminder him how much their paths had diverged. Bryn's ascent set Aidan's lack of progress into sharp relief.

Success had changed him. One of Bryn's charms in his younger days was his self-depreciating humour. He was still self-depreciating but now increasingly self-referencing, leaving no doubt that he was very proud of what he had achieved and was excited by his developing media career.

'I tell you mate, you wouldn't believe what being on TV does to a chap's pulling power. My tutorial groups are packed with some of the prettiest distractions this university can offer. It's amazing I get any work done at all. I mean this is me we're talking about here, the nerd, remember.'

Aidan didn't want to boost Bryn's self-esteem further by telling him the effect that his name had had on colleagues like Suzie. His ego did not need more massaging.

'You're not married then?' Aiden said.

'Nah. Never got around to it,' he said. 'And, to be honest, I'm having too much fun now.'

There was a knock from outside. 'Yes?' he called.

A pretty blonde girl with delightfully neat features put her head around the door.

'Hey, Bryn - oh sorry,' she said turning to look at Aidan (and dazzling him with her smile). 'Didn't realise you were busy,' she added. 'I was just wondering if you could give me ten minutes sometime next week? There are a few things that I'm still a bit hazy with for the assignment.'

'No problem, Josie... er...' Bryn was looking at the diary on his laptop. 'I'm free most of Monday morning, but not too early, right?' He flashed Josie an equally dazzling, mischievous smile back.

She giggled.

'No, not too early, please.'

'Perhaps we could do it over coffee in the café - about 10.30?' He looked enquiringly at her.

'Brilliant. See you then. Have a good weekend, Bryn.'

'You too, Josie.'

She flashed another smile at Aidan making his heart briefly skip.

'See what I mean,' said Bryn, far too pleased with himself for Aidan's liking. 'I actually have to be very careful - well careful not to get caught at least.'

Aidan laughed along with him but decided that he hated this version of Bryn. It made it much easier to use him for the main purpose of his visit.

No time like the present, he thought.

'Hey,' he said suddenly, as if just remembering something. 'You might actually be able to help me with a story I've been working on. I came across a couple of names of people I think might have worked here at some time.'

'A story, eh? Sounds intriguing. Tell me more.'

'It's nothing exciting,' said Aidan, deliberately trying to play it down. 'Just some dull business thing.'

'Well, still, always glad to help. What are their names?'

'There's one who might have been at the Business School.'

'It's a joint venture with Manchester Uni so I might have.'

'Oh right. I had thought your paths wouldn't have crossed given that he isn't a scientist.'

'Meaning that the other one is then?'

Bryn was as shrewd as ever, for all of his new playboy front.

'Well yes, I think so, but I'm not even sure that the second one ever worked here. Anyway the one I know did is someone called Mitchell Finch.'

Bryn's reaction surprised Aidan. He gave an explosive laugh.

'Mitchell Finch? What, flashy Finchy? Bloody hell, what he got himself mixed up with now?'

'You know him then?'

'Bryn pulled a face. 'Well saying I know him would be stretching a point a bit. I came across him, yes. I sat on a couple of committees that he was on too, the library board, things like that, admin stuff. He was also on an internal validation panel for a degree programme we were setting up. You couldn't miss Finch, he always wanted everyone to know he was there.'

'He was loud then?'

'No, not as such, just bloody ambitious, determined to get to the top. He didn't really have the talent to get there on merit so he substituted toadyism instead. If there was something that the Vice-Chancellor wanted doing he volunteered for it. He upset a lot of people yet he was funny and quite sad with it afterward. If he found out he upset someone he would hunt them down and apologise. He'd explain that he was having to be that way because someone in authority wanted it and he was just acting on orders.' Bryn laughed at the memory. 'I'd forgotten, he'd developed a nickname. He'd have done his nut if he'd ever found out about it. God, it was in bad taste.'

'What was it?'

Bryn pulled a face, an embarrassed wince. 'It was really bad. I don't think I should say.'

'Go on, tell me. It won't go further.'

'It had better not do.'

'You know me, Bryn.'

I do, unfortunately,' sighed Bryn. 'Oh, okay, it was Eichmann.'

'Eichmann?'

'You know, the Nazi, the final solution. I vas just vollowing orders,' he continued in a cod German accent. 'God it was cruel. Poor Mitchell. He was such a dumb ass.'

'What happened to him?'

Bryn hesitated, his face suddenly serious. 'Well... he left.'

'Why?'

'There was some scandal. Something that he'd got himself involved with. It must have been bad because he'd got tenure here. That's a job for life you know. He'd have been mad to leave for any other reason.'

'What was it? Sex?'

'No. That wouldn't have been enough; it had to be something a lot worse, something that really affected the university and reflected on its activities.'

'You have any idea what it was?'

Bryn looked uncomfortable. 'There were rumours. Look, Aidan, I have a responsibility to my university. I have to work here, remember and, for all its faults, it's a pretty good place to be. Tell me honestly, you're not doing a story on us are you?'

'No. Absolutely not. It's an investigation I'm doing into a private company. Their names came up.'

'Names? Oh yes, you said there were two. Who was the other one?'

'Gerhard Beck. Ever heard of him? I think he's German but I'm not exactly sure.'

Bryn looked thoughtful. 'That would fit,' he conceded. 'I do know that there was an overseas academic involved. But, if it is the same man, he was at the University, not UMIST.'

'So what did they do? Some sort of fraud?'

Bryn looked up sharply. 'You're fishing aren't you? You have no idea what this is all about. What are you up to, Aidan? This sounds like muck raking. We don't need that. I don't need that.'

'Bryn, honestly, I'm not doing a story on the University.'

'You sure? I'm on track for a chair, I don't want to screw that up. You do understand my position, don't you?'

Yes, I do understand it, thought Aidan. You're developing the Bryn Parry brand and you don't want to do anything to jeopardise it.

'Yes I understand. I'm not going to do anything to hurt you or UMIST. Look, as I said, these two names came up out of the blue in the middle of an investigation into a company with some... er... questions about its practices and... the honesty of its owners. Finch and Beck were listed as directors of a company that's linked to the company that I was looking at. It came as a surprise when my investigations suggested they had an academic background. It doesn't seem to fit. I'm just trying to understand where they fit in, put the pieces of the jigsaw together. Nothing more.'

Bryn stared at Aidan. He stared quite a long time. Aidan was not sure whether he was trying to tell from his face whether Aidan was lying or whether he was just weighing up what to say, whether to commit himself. Aidan willed him to open up and tried to keep calm on the surface.

'No,' he said at last. 'I don't know much and it would be unfair of me to pass on what I know; it's just hearsay and rumour. All I'll say is that the pair were reckless, got caught and got fired.'

'So they were working together?' said Aidan, trying to mask his disappointment.

'Yes they were,' said Bryn, slowly and carefully as if testing whether he was being drawn into a trap.

'But they were from totally different departments.'

'Cross disciplinary work isn't uncommon.'

'I suppose not. But Finch is, or was, a business lecturer and Beck was a...?'

He left the line hanging in the hope that Bryn would bite and finish it. He took the bait.

'A neuroscientist, yes.'

Aidan nodded in agreement as if he knew this already. Neuroscientist; interesting. The plot thickened.

'That's still an unusual match-up though, isn't it?'

Bryn just shrugged. He seemed to Aidan to be totally clamming up. He decided to take a lesson from Suzie.

'Bryn, please. I need more. The genie is out of the bottle now. I'm going to keep digging now but it would be better if I got information from someone reliable. It would be unattributable. It wouldn't get back to you. No one would know.'

'I'd know, Aidan, I'd know.' His words were spoken quietly but they had a finality about them. 'Now, I know I said that we'd go for a drink but I've actually got to do some marking tonight. Really sorry, I need a clear head. You mind taking a rain check?'

'Oh, no, no, of course not,' said Aidan, thrown a little off-balance. 'I'll hold you to that promise. It has been far too long.'

'It has, it has,' Bryn was on his feet, heading pointedly towards the door which he held open. 'I'll call you when things are a little less frantic here.'

And before he knew it, Aidan was out in the corridor and heading towards the exit.

He couldn't believe it, he'd been thrown out. His friend had actually thrown him out. And what had he gained by potentially losing a mate? Not very much. He already known that Finch and Beck had worked together, he had already guessed that Beck was some kind of scientist. A neuroscientist though; okay, he hadn't known that. That was interesting but then it still didn't lead anywhere obvious. There was and still nothing obvious to link the man through to Urbania. Actually, as he thought about it, he realised that there was still nothing to link any of the people to the accident. All they had to go on were his suspicions, backed up by Suzie admittedly, but still little more than that. Perhaps they were seeing far too much in all this.

He found himself desperately wanting a cigarette, even though he'd given up for more than a year now.

He headed towards his car fighting his cravings.

He saw the black BMW was parked two rows back from him in the university's visitors' car park. A burly man was just getting into the passenger seat. He had the build and expression of someone who worked security, menace and danger in every movement he made. He had a broad chest, tree trunk like arms and close-cropped hair with scars on his scalp visible even from a distance. Here was a man whose life was clearly lived in violence and confrontation.

Aidan's stomach tightened. So this was who was following him.

If it was intended to frighten him then it was working.

As he got to his car he had a moment of guilt. He'd brought them to Bryn. If they'd followed him in, they'd know who he'd met. He looked back, wondering whether he should warn Bryn.

But then he shrugged. There was nothing he do now, and anyway, if he got a beating, Aidan was sure that Bryn would get some decent publicity out of it that might add a nought to his next media contract. And little blonde Josie might give him some special sympathy. He smiled at this.

He got into his car and drove home. The black BMW followed him all the way.

Chapter Fifteen

Aiden's landline was ringing and when he got into his flat. He answered it.

It was Suzie and she was angry.

'Where the bloody hell have you been?'.

'And hello to you too,' said Aidan.

'I've been calling you all fucking afternoon. I thought we were meeting.'

He looked at his watch. It was nearly 6 pm. She had a point. He'd forgotten.

'Sorry Suzie, something came up.'

'And you couldn't give me a call to tell me? You just turn your mobile off? And wander off somewhere? Is that what it's going to be like working with you?'

'Are you always going to be like this?'

'If you're going to keep avoiding me, yes.'

'I wasn't avoiding you. I was in a meeting. I had to turn it off.'

'A meeting? Who with?'

He knew he was in trouble but couldn't think of a way out other than by admitting the truth.

'Bryn Parry,' he said quite quietly. There was a brief pause at the other end of the line. He waited for the explosion. He didn't have to long to wait.

'Bryn Parry? You went to see Bryn Parry on your own? You knew that I wanted to go with you.'

'Yes, but-'

'But you just bloody well went and did it all the same without bloody telling me. You don't trust me then, Aidan, is that it?'

Yes, he thought.

'No,' he said.

'Then why the hell did you do it?'

'It came out of the blue. I called an old number. I didn't think I'd get through but I did and then he invited me straight over.'

'That doesn't explain why you didn't call me.'

'Hey, come on I have a brain too. I don't need you to hold my hand,' Aidan tried shifting from defence to anger. 'Don't forget Bryn isn't just any old contact, he's my friend. It would have looked odd going along mob handed. He'd have thought we were after something.'

'We were after something,' Suzie pointed out.

'Well, yes, but I thought I'd try a less obvious approach.'

'We could still have done that. You could have introduced me as your girlfriend.'

Aidan could not help but give a snort of laughter. 'Yes, he'd really believe that,' he said.

There was a brief silence from the other end of the line.

'Anyway, what did you find out?' she said at last.

He hesitated, partly because he wasn't sure just what he'd actually discovered but also because a disturbing thought had come to mind and now wouldn't go away.

'Not on here.'

'What do you mean, not on here?'

'I'd prefer to tell you face-to-face.'

Another pause.

'Why?' she said at last.

'Can't you just accept not hearing for now?'

'I don't see why I should.'

'Just trust me, can't you?'

'No I can't, Aidan.'

'Why not?'

'Because you're a real piece of work. Just tell me.'

'No.'

'Suit yourself.'

The phone abruptly went dead. She'd rung off.

Aidan held the receiver to his lips for a minute before putting it down.

'Bloody hell,' he muttered to himself.

He looked at the handset of his landline. It would be odd if they had gone to the trouble of hacking into his voicemail and burgling his flat and yet not done anything about his phone.

The more he thought about it, the more likely was that they had done. He had meant to check but had not had the time. It was only when talking to Suzie that he remembered. Well now was a chance to find out.

He turned on the TV and put on the football to cover the noise he was going to make and went into the kitchen. In his bit drawer he found a small selection of screwdrivers. He didn't really have one ideally suited to the fine, Phillips type screws that held the back but he managed to persuade the tip of a small knife to fit, and, ignoring the shavings of aluminium produced and the warning label that told him his guarantee will be invalidated should he remove the cover, he pulled the phone apart.

He wasn't an expert, he wasn't sure what should have been in there but he was pretty certain what shouldn't, and into that category fell the tiny microphone attached to a sliver of electronic circuit board complete with a small cat's whisker of an aerial.

Aidan looked at the bug for some time, weighing up what was the least worst option and also trying to remember what he had just said to Suzie. Was it something that could be used against him? Again and again he found himself wishing that his memory was better. In the end he decided that it would be best if he put the phone back together, but took a series of photographs with his Polaroid clearly showing the device on tonight's edition of the paper showing the date.

He looked around the flat. Would there be other bugs? They had hacked his mobile and his flat's phone, would they really stop at that? Where would the bugs be? He was no expert but the phone device looked very professional so they'd probably have done an equally good job in concealing the rest. He made a half-hearted search but found nothing. Despite this, Aidan had no doubts that they were there.

He was exposed. He had no privacy; every part of his life was being observed. It was a horrible feeling. But what the hell could he do about it?

He jumped to his feet; then cursed, silently, trying to act normally just in case they were watching.

Shit, this was suffocating, terrifying, followed everywhere, watched even at home.

He needed to get out of this straitjacket. But where could he go even if could get out of here? Roisin's? Possibly but they hadn't exactly parted on good terms last time.

So where else? Most of his other friends were now married, many of those with children. The open houses he had enjoyed in the early years of working were now closed to him as, one by one, they'd vanished into family life.

He had nowhere to go.

A hotel then? He winced at that thought; even the cheapest budget chain hotel charged a far higher rate for a short while. It might actually feel like a holiday.

But, at the end of it, would anything have changed if he made no progress? The bugs would still be here, he'd be followed again.

In the background, the football match had reached half-time and pundits on headphones were discussing the saints and sinners of the game using umpteen slow motion replays. He couldn't care less.

He thought about going to the police again. It was an option, but there was another.

There was Suzie. He needed to crack the story so he needed her help. Would she be willing? Their last conversation did not bode well but, given the circumstances, perhaps she would. But, pay as you go mobile or not, how could he contact her without being overheard or being followed when he left the flat?

A text on his 'clean' mobile would sort out the former but he still needed to get away from here unseen.

Aidan looked out of his lounge window. The evening was overcast and an early twilight had fallen as a result. Good, the gloom would help but he'd leave it an hour or so to make sure it was getting properly dark.

There were four flats on each the floor of his block, three floors, twelve flats in all. He was on the back looking out over the car park, the exit to his right. There was a fence all round the block, except the side with the entrance to the car park. The fence was tall, eight feet at least, the type with wooden panels fitting into grooves in the concrete posts. The fence on the left side of the car park ran alongside a gully, hiding an urban stream. He knew that there was a footpath by the stream because he had seen schoolchildren take a shortcut through the flat's car park. They'd lifted up one of the panels and scrambled underneath it.

The loose fence panel was out of sight just beyond the bin store. The men who were watching the flats would probably not be able to see that corner from where they were parked. Even if they did, he could be through it and away along the path before they could react.

He got a rucksack and stuffed a change of clothes, fresh underwear and basic toiletries into it, plus laptop, notebooks, mobile charger and camera - all the tools of the working journalist. He decided to empty the bins, partly because he did not know when he would be back and partly to giving cover to go out to the bin store.

He then sat and pretended to watch the match as the room darkened. At last he could stand it no longer.

He looked around the flat. He would have to leave the TV on for a while so they would not get too suspicious. He worked through the TV's remote control, he found a sleep setting. He set it for two hours which he thought was a reasonable time to stay up until. Satisfied, he picked up the bag of rubbish and his rucksack and padded slowly and softy to the door. Very quietly, he stepped outside pulling the door gently to after him, wincing as it clicked loudly into place. Then, with exaggerated slowness, he inserted the key into the mortice lock and turned it.

'Mr Hughes. What are you doing?'

The voice right behind him made him jump. He turned, then breathed again.

'Hello, Mrs Doherty.'

She was one of his neighbours, a retiree who Aidan had long believed had some of the sharpest hearing in Christendom. She had cracked open her front door and was peering around it.

'I heard someone creeping around,' she said.

'Yes, well it was me,' said Aidan, not knowing what else to say.

'There are some funny types around,' she said. 'We can never be too careful. I see that you had the police around.' The words were a clear accusation.

'Yes I had burglars,' he said. 'I don't suppose you heard anything?'

'When?'

No words of sympathy then, Aidan noted.

'It was yesterday. Some time in the day.'

'I'm at work all day, you can't expect working folk to be able to keep an eye on things.'

Aidan remembered that Mrs Doherty worked in a charity shop. He always wondered whether they would make more money without her. He was sure that she must frighten their customers. She frightened him.

'No... well I...,' he lifted up his bag of rubbish indicating where he was headed but saw her eyes stray to his rucksack.

'You're going out?'

'Yes, for a little while.'

'You've left your TV on.'

'Yes I have.'

'You must have money to burn.'

'I'm worried about burglars.'

Mrs Doherty looked affronted. 'Well there's no need to worry about it when people are in. We all look out for each other here. I hear everything.'

'Yes, well. I'm still going to leave it on,' he said, turning towards the stairs.

Mrs Doherty was persistent.

'You should think of others and turn it off.'

'And you should fucking well mind your own business.'

Aidan hadn't meant to either yell or swear but he'd seen red. He felt terrible, like he'd just sworn at his own mother.

'I'm sorry,' said Aidan but now to the outside of a slammed door. He thought briefly of knocking and apologising but then thought better of it. It was good if the old witch kept away from him.

He headed out to the bin store, the bin bag held away from his body. He looked towards the road; he could see the bonnet of the BMW but that was all. It seemed to be the same car every time, Aidan wondered whether it was the same pair all the time or whether there were shifts of watchers.

Then he wondered why he was getting concerned about the welfare of those who were intruding into his life.

He opened the heavy lid of the large wheeled bin and tossed the bag inside. Then without hesitating but feeling very self-conscious, he walked around the back of the store to the fence. He stood behind it for a moment. He was in the deep shadows, light from the street lamps not penetrating this far. This was good but made finding the right panel difficult. He tugged ineffectually at several without shifting them an inch. In the end he had to risk using his lighter, which he still carried despite him supposedly being a non-smoker now,to find the right panel, the one with a broken fastenings.

Getting his fingers underneath it. he found it slid up quite easily, though it was very heavy, and slid straight down again when left. Aidan now recalled that when he had seen the school kids use this route has always been at least two of them out of it in turns to hold up the panel. He wasn't sure how he was going to do this. In the end he found he pushed the panels up far enough it would wedge at an angle. It was precarious, it fell with the first time he left it alone with a dull thud that reverberated across the car park. This caused at least one person to peer out of their flat's windows and spurred Aidan into one last effort to get through.

He wedged the panel into place again; this time it held. Aidan scrabbled through, scratching his face on the brambles and felt the cold gritty ooze of mud on his hands and through the knees of his trousers. He was afraid the panel would fall on the back of his neck like a blunt guillotine but it didn't; it fell on the back of his legs and pinned him in a very awkward position. Panicking, Aidan had visions of being stuck there all night and found the morning with his ankles and feet purple from lack of circulation and this notion causing to squirm and tug first one and then the other leg free of the fence. All he had to do then was push the panel back up to retrieve the trainer that he had lost on the other side. As he did, his hand and the trainer were illuminated in the beam of a torch and a deep voice rang out.

'Oy! What the hell do you think you're doing? I've called the police, they're on the way.'

Aidan was relieved that the voice came from the flat side of the fence. He thought it was the builder who live in the flat below his. He wasn't going to stay to find out and felt about for his rucksack.

'Bloody kids! You just bloody wait till I catch you!'

To Aidan's horror the fence panel started to slide up. Quickly, he hobbled away down the dark path as quickly as he could, stumbling once, falling on in his face.

It wasn't until he reached the end of the path and the lights of the main road that he felt safe again. He was breathing hard, covered in mud and his calves were stinging like the devil but he was pleased with himself. He had done it, he had slipped away from the flat unobserved.

Well mainly unobserved. Not by anyone important though.

A major triumph, he thought savagely, well done.

Now for the next stage. As he walked towards the tram stop he took out his new mobile and called Suzie.

'Hello. I got your text. What do you want?'

She was still angry then.

'Look, I'm sorry. I had good reason not to speak on the landline.'

'Pull the other one-'

'Please. Something's happened and I really need your help.'

There was a silence at the other end of the line. It lasted so long that he thought the call had dropped and checked to see if they were still connected.

'Okay,' she said at last. 'What do you want?'

He breathed a long sigh of relief. 'Well, for a start I need somewhere to stay.

Chapter Sixteen

May 7th 1997 9.50pm

They settled on meeting at the pub close to the house that Suzie shared with Samantha - Sam.

Suzie laughed when she saw him.

'What the hell have you been up to, Aidan? Playing in the bushes?'

'Very funny. I need to go and clean up. Get me a drink please.'

He headed for the gents. In the toilets, looking in the mirror, he could understand her laughter; his face was covered in mud, he had scratches on his cheek and his shirt and jeans were filthy. He ran water into the sink and cleaned himself up as best as he could then went back to find her.

She sat on her own in a quiet corner of the lounge bar, two long glasses on the table in front of her, one slightly less full than the other.

'You didn't say what you wanted,' she said, 'so I got you the same as me.'

'Thanks,' said Aidan picking up the full one and taking a sip. It was vodka and tonic. That was fine, in fact anything alcoholic would have been.

'So what's all this about? Why have you been re-enacting the Great Escape?'

'I got sick of being watched.'

'Oh come on-'

'I'm being followed everywhere and my flat has been bugged.'

'Yeah right,' Suzie looked at him incredulously. 'You're getting paranoid.'

'Am I?' He handed over the Polaroids. 'That's the bug on my phone.'

She looked at them in shocked silence.

'Good God,' she said at last. 'Sorry, I thought you're overreacting. I was angry too.'

'I was hardly playing for the team this afternoon was I?'

'No you weren't. And would you have been here if it wasn't for this?' She held up one of the Polaroids.

'Yes, I would.'

'Yeah, sure you would Aidan, sure you would.'

The atmosphere chilled again. But eventually it was Suzie who broke the silence. 'Look, if we are going to get anywhere with this then have to work together. Properly, agreed?'

'Agreed.'

'Good. So what did you find out this afternoon?'

Relieved to have got off lightly, Aidan pulled out his notebook and went over what Bryn told him. He had scribbled some notes down whilst everything was still fresh in his mind, sat in the car outside his flat before going up. Suzie's reaction was very similar to what his own had been.

'That's interesting,' she said. 'But where does it fit into the story?'

'I don't know,' admitted Aidan. 'Other than that car registration there's nothing else to link Finch and Beck with Urbania or to Mickey Smith. It just looks like a totally different company, a different story. But something tells me that this is something we can't just ignore.'

Suzie nodded thoughtfully.

'Your journalistic instincts? Well to be honest, mine are working overtime too. You think your friend Parry knows more?'

'I'm sure he does,' said Aidan. 'I thought he was about to tell me something but changed his mind.'

'We need to go back to him, put the pressure on.'

'No.'

'No? Come on Aidan, this is a lead.'

'That's not the right way with Bryn, I know him, remember? Bryn worked out I was fishing. He didn't want to be the primary source. Let's leave it a couple of days, build up the background, hope to pick up something definite and then go back.'

Suzie looked like she was going to argue but then nodded. 'Alright.'

'So what have you found?'

Suzie took a deep breath, as if weighing something up. 'You said we're partners, right? In this together? No hiding things from each other?' he said.

That seemed to trigger the decision in her.

'Okay, you're right. Quid pro quo,' she said. 'Well, as you know, this isn't the first time I've been involved with looking at Mickey Smith and his brother. Richard and I did four years ago, concentrating on Mickey as he's the linchpin of it all.'

Aidan nodded.

'Yes,' he said. 'I got that impression.'

She nodded. 'Richard got worked up about Smith, he was determined to get him. He built up a huge dossier on him, all paper, nothing electronic, he was paranoid about that. And with good reason; Mickey Smith is a really nasty piece of work, he's capable of anything.'

'So what happened? Why didn't you and Richard publish?'

Susie took another deep breath before answering. She seemed to be using the time to weigh up what she was going to say. Aidan tried to be patient.

'We should have. Richard and I had a big argument about it,' she said at last. 'I thought we had enough to go but he was dead against it. This was just after that Urbania article was published. It was meant to be a first exposé, a teaser, the one that was going to get people to come out into the open but...well, it just didn't happen. No one came forward, no disgruntled ex-employee in the know and then, after Richard had done a last bit of digging, he came to me one day and just pulled it.'

'What?'

'I know. Imagine how I felt. I was…well it's hard to describe how I was; furious, upset, frustrated. I still thought we had enough but Richard said we hadn't, that all we had was circumstantial, that if we went to press with it we'd be crucified, that we'd both be out of a job and all that.'

Suzie was staring at the floor as she spoke, obviously deep in thought, remembering. She had also spoken softly, reflectively, seriously. Aidan said nothing, not wanting to interrupt her train of thought.

'The thing was it was so unlike him. He'd been so enthusiastic, you know what he was like, and single-minded.'

Aidan nodded. 'Yup,' he said.

'He'd come to hate Mickey Smith, it became more than just a story, much more,' she continued. She shook her head. 'But he just stopped, stopped the whole lot; wanted the dossier burned, stood over me whilst I did it. And then he stopped seeing me.'

Suzie abruptly glanced up, looking at Aidan like she'd been caught doing something wrong. She didn't mean to admit to that, he guessed.

He tried to come to her aid.

'Any idea why he pulled the plug?'

She took a sip of her drink before answering.

'I thought he'd got frightened, that he was getting old, past it. I'm afraid I told him that.'

'You don't think that now?'

She shook her head. 'Richard wasn't someone who did age, was he? That was part of his charm, that he never seemed to grow up.'

Aidan nodded.

'So why didn't you go on yourself? You'd looked at the same stuff?'

'Yes but I didn't have Richard. I was a trainee, just out of uni. I needed his clout. Once it had gone…' She sighed. 'But now it looks like he did have another go.'

'And it killed him,' muttered Aidan.

Suzie nodded.

'It looks like it,' she said. 'So what now?'

'If only we had Richard's dossier.' said Aidan.

Suzie stared at him for a few moment. 'Well,' she said at last. 'Actually, I do have it.'

'What? How?'

'Richard kept it at mine.'

'But you destroyed it.'

She smiled. 'He made the mistake of telling me what he wanted to do with it before he came over.'

'So you burned–'

'Three years of university notes stuffed into the box files.'

'Can I see it?'

She nodded. 'Yes. You'll have to. But where? Not at your place, obviously. Nor the office. You've got to go to ground.'

'What? Oh…right. They'd follow me again.'

Suzie smiled. 'The penny's dropped. Looks like you'll be negotiating some leave. Or going sick.'

Aidan nodded. 'Can I stay at yours?'

'At mine? I don't think so. It wouldn't be fair on Sam.'

'Where then?'

Suzie frowned. 'Not at a hotel, they'd check, same with a B&B, unless you paid cash of course, I wouldn't put it past them being able to check credit cards.' She bit her lip thoughtfully. 'There is one place I know, but you'd have to promise to look after it.'

'Where?'

'My aunt and uncle's house in Sale. They are doing a round the world retirement trip, three months, spending the grey pound. I'm keeping an eye on the place, watering the plants.

But,' she added. 'Damage it and I'll damage you, understand?'

Aidan nodded.

'I'll go and get the dossier get my car and take you there.' She drained her drink. 'Back in ten.'

Before he could say anything she was gone, leaving him to come to terms with what was going to happen.

He was doing this. He was actually doing it.

Gill would be furious with him, she wouldn't agree to leave, not with him being the only business staffer left, so he'd be going off sick. But now he had somewhere safe to live, somewhere to work on the story.

THE story.

Make or break.

This was good.

Wasn't it?

Chapter Seventeen

May 8th 1997 8.20am

Aidan woke late to an unfamiliar soundtrack; birdsong.

Suzie's aunt and uncle lived in a large, detached house in a leafy suburb. She had told him he could sleep anywhere but he'd chosen the box room because it reminded him of his own childhood bedroom. There, in the comfort of a soft, deep duvet, the stress of the previous few days had melted away and he'd slept well for the first time since the accident.

After a long, leisurely shower he hunted out some breakfast and ran up against the first problem; there was virtually no food in the house, hardly surprising given the householder's long trip. He found some instant coffee, stale with age, a tin of baked beans and some crispbreads. They would do until he went shopping.

As he ate he started to read the dossier.

It was comprised of a box file packed full of foolscap notes, printed A4 paper and news clippings, comprising some 500 pages in total and under a single title in Richard's best block capitals; 'The Smith Family.' It consisted of sections delineated by coloured dividers. The sections were Family/Background; Illegal Activities, subdivided into Protection, Drugs, People smuggling, Prostitution and Slave Labour; and Legal Activities/ Public Face which had three sub-sections - Property, Security and Casinos.

This was typically Richard; thorough and organised. Aidan smiled, typical of his journalism anyway, a total contrast to his disorganised personal life. It was like he'd put so much into the former there was nothing left over for the latter. The pang of loss came back and the smile faded. He could smell the cigarette smoke and the whisky impregnating every page. This was Richard's memorial and he had to honour it.

Rather than skip to the meaty stuff, he was going to go through it in order, and carefully.

He started to read from the very start.

He was glad he did; he learned much about the Smiths from it.

The boy's father and uncle owned a scrapyard and, even in their day, this was widely believed to be a cover for a wide range of illegal activity. The older Smiths were bruisers and enforcers, the boy's uncle having convictions for GBH, receiving stolen goods, running a car ringing gang and, finally, manslaughter following a bar fight. The other, father to Peter and Mickey, led a more charmed life, charged and tried for a whole series of crimes, usually getting off or, at worst, having the conviction overturned on appeal. Nothing would stick.

Until his temper got the better of him.

It was a long-standing dispute with a neighbour over a hedge at Smith's house that brought him down. The man, a retired engineer in his 70s, refused to be cowed by Smith and his heavies and had Smith's hedge trimmed as it was overshadowing his garden. Smith Sr had taken a baseball bat and smashed his neighbour's skull to a pulp - pieces of bone and brain were found all over Smith including in his hair - and the police, called by the engineer's wife, arrived before he could flee.

So the scrapyard and, presumably, the crime empire was passed to the sons, Peter and Mickey.

Peter seemed to be a typical Smith, in trouble with the police since the age of ten, serving his first custodial sentence at fourteen, continuing in the same vein until his twenties. Aidan guessed that Richard had a source with access to criminal records for Peter's record seemed to have been paraphrased from legalese. The - extensive - record revealed that Peter

Smith seemed to specialise in violent or stupid crimes, often both, being caught numerous times because his temper got the better of him and there was no chance of denying what he'd done. He was clearly all muscle rather than brain.

Certainly not a natural master criminal.

Unlike Mickey.

He had just one caution on his juvenile record. When he was twelve he'd beaten up a schoolmate, admittedly so badly that the boy's jaw had to be wired up and there were fears that he might lose the sight in one eye. But after that there was nothing. It was like Mickey had vanished off the face of the earth.

He made notes as he went and here it read 'Where did Mickey go?'. Richard had obviously thought the same because it was written in the margins of the very next page. He'd found the answer too; Mickey had gone to school, and not just any school but a posh one, private, fee paying.

Aidan shook his head as he read this. Everything had been as he'd expected until this.

Richard had been surprised too and had done a lot of digging, even going as far as interviewing a couple of Mickey's former schoolmates. They'd both said much the same thing, that Mickey was very clever but didn't mix much. He was quiet and reserved but, as one said, "You always got the impression he was watching everyone, scheming, making plans".

He actually got into university to study, of all things, economics but, during his first year, his father had murdered his next door neighbour and Mickey had left, never to return.

And now Mickey Smith really faded away. The background section ended with two facts; firstly Mickey was married with two children, both themselves at private schools, and lived in millionaire's row in Alderley Edge. The second was that Mickey Smith, by rumour, by feeling, by unacknowledged implication, had taken over his father and uncle's criminal businesses at the tender age of nineteen.

There were also a couple of photos; one taken at school, the other looking like a more recent long-lens surveillance shot.

There was no doubt now. Mickey Smith was the driver.

But that was not enough now, was it? All the other evidence had gone, Aidan had left it too late to take this to the police and it was looking like it was a minor episode, despite the death involved.

They needed more.

He read on.

At the start of the Illegal Activities section, Richard had gone to the paper's archive, covering a period sixteen years before, consisting of photocopies of the microfiche of back articles. It concentrated on a fairly short period; the six weeks immediately following the father's arrest, and covered a wave of violence; shootings, beatings, mutilations and took place all over Salford and Greater Manchester. There were some editorial comments about how the area was becoming the gun and gang capital of Britain. Some of the news articles carried Richard's own by-line, probably from the very start of his career. He had then just reported the bald facts; '35 year-old man shot dead in gangland style execution' and '28 year-old man's hand hacked off in machete attack' were just two examples. Now his notes showed that four years ago he had looked deeper, at who these men were, where their families came from, who their associates were, their criminal records and the like. Richard had produced a chart which summarised all of this. If it was accurate - and, knowing Richard, it would be - then it was clear that every major crime family in the area had suffered short, sharp and brutal shocks. Richard's conclusions were clear; the potential power vacuum and potential turf war caused by the removal of his father had been nipped in the bud ruthlessly and efficiently. Although there was no proof, there was only one possible candidate who had the intelligence and drive to carry this through.

Mickey Smith.

Fear swept over Aidan like a tidal wave.

Shit.

This was the man he'd flipped the bird at. The one who he'd pissed off so much that he'd provoked into road rage.

'Fuck, fuck, fuck! What have I done?'

Aidan got to his feet - too quickly because the room dimmed and he staggered, having to hold onto the table to stop himself falling.

It took a few seconds to recover his balance and his vision to return to normal. He wondered whether he should run, go to the airport, fly anywhere as long it was outside the country.

He took some deep breaths. He needed to calm himself. It was probably too late to run, Mickey probably had the reach to catch him anywhere.

He was committed to this. He had to take Smith down. It was his only choice.

But it was a crazy choice.

Who did he think he was? He wasn't Woodward and Bernstein; he was Aidan Hughes, crap business correspondent of a regional newspaper eight years into a career going absolutely nowhere.

Maybe finding a tall building like Richard was the best option…

No.

He went and made himself a coffee. He wasn't alone now. He had Suzie. She was good. Yes, he was slightly scared of her but that was good; if he found her intimidating so would others.

These thoughts - and the caffeine - calmed him.

It was still a quarter of an hour before he was able to go back to his reading.

* * *

May 8th 1997 2.15pm

By mid-afternoon he'd made a lot of progress through the dossier.

He didn't feel any better.

The Illegal Activities section - the people smuggling, protection racket, slave labour and prostitution - become more general, mainly because Mickey Smith kept things at a careful distance from himself.

There was a note in Richard's handwriting that revealed his own frustration; 'Can we link this to MS?'

The answer seemed to be 'No', at least in any attributable way.

There were transcripts from two interviews. By the look of it separate informers but both made it clear that they were not going on the record and that they were not going to speak on tape.

The fact that the transcripts existed showed that either Richard or Suzie had lied and had worn a wire.

Aidan wondered if he'd have the balls to do that.

The first transcript was from someone just referred to as 'D'. There were a couple of quotes, one of which read: 'Mickey Smith is clever. Clever, careful and ruthless. He's always kept a distance from operations, kept his hands clean. He's the puppet master, if one of his puppets gets caught then the strings are cut.'

That made sense. But there was another, longer transcript that showed a different story, one where Mickey did get involved but in a way that would make anyone taking it to the authorities unlikely.

The transcript was of a long conversation with someone referred to as 'H'.

H - He's got a temper though, Mickey has. I heard this one story when he really lost it. He got pushed too far, someone close to him, just outside the inner circle but close enough, had gone into business for his self.

Int - That was a risk wasn't it?

H - Yeah, well, everyone did it, there was so much cash sloshing around it were easy. Mickey knew it too, it were like a perk that you'd pocket the odd ten or twenty now and again. Then there were the girls, they were lookers, eastern European, Chinese, gorgeous little things. Couldn't help but have a freebie every now and then, you know.

Int - So why…?

H - I were telling you. Well this guy went too far wi' it. He started bragging about what he did, how he were going to be the next big boss, that he could do what he liked. Well, that were it, Mickey weren't having that, was he?'

Int - So what happened?

H - Well like I said, I weren't there, I just heard, right?

Int - Yes. You said, You weren't there. So what happened?

H - Mickey had him lifted from the street. He was just going to have 'im worked over. That's all but the git wouldn't shut up, would he? He were one of them, Koran on Friday, lap dancing on Saturday, used to throwing his weight around. He started cursin' Mickey, saying things about Mickey's wife, how she could do with a real man and that he'd do the business sometime. Well, that got back to Mickey and he just blew.

Int - What happened? What did Mickey do?

H - He sorted him out. Let's just leave it like that, eh?

Int - Come on. You weren't there, it's only hearsay, right? How can it hurt?

H - Why should I?

Int - Well, for one thing because we're fucking paying you and what you've given me so far is shit. Come on, it can't get back to you, you know that. It just gives me something to follow up on.

H - Yeah, well…

Int - Look, it's probably nothing we've not heard before..

H - If you've heard it then why do you need me?

Int - If we don't hear it from you why should I pay you the rest, eh? I'm not fucking paying for sod all.

H - [Inaudable]

Int - What was that, H?

H - I said he crucified him.

Int - Well, we knew he beat him…

H - You aint fucking listening, are you? He crucified him, with a nail gun, really fucking crucified him up against this wall, hands and feet, the works. The poor cunt was squealing like a pig. Then Mickey…

Int - Then Mickey what?

H - Then he tore the guy's balls off. Literally fxxxxx tore them off with his bare hands and stuffed them in the poor fxxxxx mouth. I were sick but Mickey loved it, he were laughing.

Int - You were sick?

H - What?

Int - You said you were sick. You were there, weren't you?

H - No I weren't. I neva was. I just heard, right? Now I want my fucking money and I want it now. And you can fuck off, I neva want to see you round here again, okay.

Int - Yes but…

H - Yeah but nowt. That's yer lot. You better not have been wearing a wire. Hey, you haven't have you because…

Int - No wire, I said… [Muffled] Hey, what are you…stop.

INTERVIEW ENDS.

Aidan swallowed hard. This was even worse than he thought. It was like he was in a slow motion nightmare.

He had another coffee.

* * *

May 8th 1997 6.35pm

Suzie arrived in the evening after Aidan was getting to the end of the last third of the dossier, the part that dealt with the Smith family legitimate businesses.

'God, I'm sweaty,' she said. 'And you look like I did after I first read that. I'm going for a shower. I've brought some beers, help yourself and crack one open for me would you?'

Aidan did, then went back to finish his reading.

The security business had become huge and, in many ways, was an understandable extension of a crime business; what better way to utilize big, heavy, violent men? It also had crossovers with other aspects of the business providing door cover at pubs and clubs and security patrols for the property enterprise, Urbania. It allowed the other side of the property business, the part that started under Smith senior, the slum landlord enterprise, to be squeezed of every drop of income. Property was, again, an obvious add-on to crime; it could swallow huge amounts of dirty money and launder it nicely.

So, too, could the casino business but thereby hung a mystery; how did an organisation with links to organised crime get a licence? Richard's notes clearly showed he felt the same, and his frustration that he could not see why they had showed through. Aidan could see why, okay, there was no direct proof that Mickey Smith was bent, he had no convictions, but surely the question should have been asked.

So why wasn't it?

He sipped his beer. He'd been in one of the casinos mentioned in the dossier last year at a stag do. Then he remembered something else; Richard had been invited too but had refused to go. That had been odd, Richard loved a flutter and was a great poker and blackjack player. Aidan hadn't been able to fathom why he wouldn't jump at the chance to go to the casino.

Now the reason was obvious; Richard did not want to put his money into Mickey Smith's wallet.

Suzie came downstairs towelling her long, dark hair and wearing a tracksuit bearing the badge of the local hockey club. Aidan realised that she probably used her uncle and aunt's place as a useful base if she was a member, hence the change of clothes.

'That mine?' she said, nodding at the other bottle. She took it and took a swig before he'd answered. 'So, what do you think?'

'Terrifying,' he said, 'and puzzling.'

'What is?'

'There's so much evidence here. Why didn't Richard act on it?'

Suzie pulled a face. 'There were…reasons,' she said quietly.

'But this transcript with H,' he said, flicking back through the dossier to it. 'Surely if you'd gone to the police they could have…'

'They could have what? Given them protection?'

'Yes.'

Suzie leaned across him and turned a few pages in the dossier to one which contained a couple of clippings from the paper. She stabbed her finger at them. 'Did you see these?'

Aidan looked. The first was a report of a body being found in the Irwell, badly beaten and with the head and hands missing. The second was longer and dated about six weeks later and reported that, following a tip-off, police had checked the DNA of the family of Hanif Mohammed and had proved that the body was his. When Aidan had read it, he assumed that this was the body of the crucified and castrated man.

'Yes, I saw them,' he said.

'That was H,' she said. 'That was the guy we taped. He disappeared a few days after he spoke to Richard. We thought he was just lying low, had got cold feet but when he didn't show for his daughter's birthday party, Richard put two and two together and tipped off the cops.'

Aidan tried to swallow again but now it felt like he had a concrete cricket ball in his throat. Eventually he managed it.

'How did Smith find out?' he croaked. 'About H, I mean.'

Suzie shrugged. 'Who knows? Richard suspected it might be a mole in our place, even though he'd been so careful about setting up meetings, about what he was doing, where he was going, working from the office you always leave tracks, don't you? He got paranoid about it, that's why the dossier was at mine. He gathered everything together and brought it over the next day.'

'But still someone found out?'

Suzie nodded. 'They must have, though God knows how.' She sighed. 'It rocked Richard, shocked him to the core to be honest. It made him question what we'd got ourselves into.'

'I know how he feels,' said Aidan. 'But that wasn't like Richard.'

She nodded. 'No, it wasn't. He was different though, he was always a great reporter, never gave up, always willing to dig a bit further but this was different; he was obsessed. Maybe it was the lack of hard evidence, the fact that Mickey Smith always seemed to be out of reach, that affected him so much. He was convinced that it would be the legit business that brought Smith down, that he'd bring over the methods from crime and that he'd slip up. But he never did. Richard couldn't bear that.'

She was now staring thoughtfully at the dossier, like she was expecting it to suddenly give up its secrets.

'Why did he give up?' said Aidan, breaking the spell. 'Even after splitting with you and supposedly getting you to burn all this. I know Richard, he'd still go on.'

Abruptly Suzie moved away and went and stood by the patio window staring out into the garden. She looked troubled, pensive, clearly weighing something in her mind. He left her to it.

At last she seemed to come to a decision.

'I know something about Richard, a secret,' she said. 'Perhaps it doesn't matter now he's gone but…actually it does. So if I tell you it stays within these four walls, okay?'

'Yes, of course, it goes without saying.'

Though you did say it, Aidan thought.

She took a deep breath. 'When Richard joined the business desk he'd been on sick leave, remember?'

'Yes. He'd had a heart attack.'

Suzie shook her head. 'It wasn't a heart attack. He had a breakdown. He was sectioned.'

Chapter Eighteen

They took Suzie's car into town, a small hatchback which, to Aidan's surprise, was filthy inside and out. He'd somehow expected her to be neat, smart and sporty in everything but clearly this wasn't the case.

He didn't comment on it because they'd already argued about how to start the investigation.

'The key's got to be the business side,' Aidan had argued. 'That was what Richard thought.'

'Yeah, but that's a dead end without Richard. Where do we start? It could take weeks to work out what he found.'

'But-'

'But nothing. Mickey Smith is a crime boss. That's where we need to start. We need to find out what he's up to.'

He had conceded defeat this time but resolved to find a way to stand up for himself next time, which meant having better arguments prepared.

Hence this trip.

'Are you sure this guy will be there?' he said.

"This guy" was one of the sources that Richard had used, a senior member of another crime family who operated in the same murky world as the Smiths. He was also one of the few who Suzie recognised.

'Jimmy? Who knows? There's a good chance though.'

Aidan nodded. Given where they were going, there were chances other things could happen too; nasty, violent things. It was a rough area in daylight.

It would be dark when they got there.

There were things bothering him other than where they were going.

'About Richard's breakdown,' he said.

'What of it?'

'How bad was he?'

'Pretty bad. He'd been under a lot of stress, he cracked.'

'Right, so…' Aidan couldn't bring himself to say it.

Suzie was not going to let it hang; 'So? So what? Just say what you were going to.'

'So, was he in that state when he put the dossier together? Is it all the product of a disturbed mind?'

Suzie slammed the brakes on and pulled to the side of the road, much to the surprise of the driver behind who blew his horn long and loudly.

'You really are an absolute dickhead, aren't you?' she said. 'Get out. I'll do this on my own.'

Deja vu. Did he have this effect on every woman he knew? Probably he thought. Time to build bridges.

'Suzie, I was just thinking aloud.'

'Well don't.'

'But it's just what anyone we bring this to might ask. I didn't mean it to come out like that.'

'How else was it going to sound?'

'Yeah, yeah, I know. Richard was my friend too, remember. I guess I'm still in shock about it.'

Suzie still looked furious.

He leaned over, put his hand on hers. 'I am sorry. Richard was a fantastic reporter, I know that. The dossier has to be right, that's clear enough. We just need to prove that it is, link Smith to all of it. Please, Suzie, let's work together to do it. For Richard.'

Suzie puffed out her cheeks.

'The whole thing consumed him,' she said. 'Putting the dossier together took him to the edge. But something happened that pushed him over and I still don't know what.' She bit her lip. 'That was one of the reasons I never went back to it myself, even though I had it. I was worried that if he ever knew I had, he'd do the same and it would kill him.'

God, she really loved him, thought Aidan.

'Yes, I understand,' he said.

'I need to tell you something,' she muttered.

'What?'

'You need to know why I'm working with you.'

'Okay?' he said cautiously.

'It's only because you're a witness. You saw something, you can link Mickey Smith to something criminal. You're the link that could bring him down. I want to do that, for Richard.' She shrugged. 'Sorry. You needed to know.'

Aidan nodded.

That made sense. Perhaps he should be insulted and angry. He surprised himself by not being.

'I did wonder,' he said. 'Maybe I'll find a way of impressing you. Stranger things have happened.' He smiled.

Suzie did too. 'Maybe.'

'Now we've got that in the open shall we try to get these bastards?'

She nodded, looked in her mirror, put the car into gear and drove off again.

They were soon in a part of town way out of Aidan's comfort zone, in some of the roughest streets of the toughest areas. It was a different world, intimidatingly alien. It seemed every face turned to watch them pass, like everyone recognised them as intruders, outsiders.

They drove past a group of feral children.

'Where were you thinking of parking?' he said, having visions of coming back to a wheelless car up on bricks, or a stripped, burned out shell and having to make their way out on foot.

'At the Multiplex,' she said. 'It's a bit of a walk but it should be safe enough there. I just thought we'd have a look see first, see what's going on.'

She pulled up to the kerb and pointed towards a pub, a typically shabby 1970s building. 'That's Jimmy's local,' she said. 'Or was back then.'

'How do you know?'

'I came with Richard to find him once,' she said.

Aidan nodded. 'You sure he'll still drink there?'

She shrugged. 'It's as good a place as any to start. Let's hope he's a creature of habit.'

A movement out of the corner of his eye caught Aidan's attention. Two girls had stepped out of a doorway, they were long legged, short skirted, wearing cheap, glittery tops. Skeletally thin, they tottered towards the car on high heels. The fact there was a couple in the car didn't seem to bother them.

'Suzie,' he said urgently as one of the girls leaned against his door and stared in at him.

'What? Oh, right.' To his horror she lowered the window on Aidan's side. 'Not today, love,' she said. 'Maybe another time.'

'Fuck you, bitch,' said the girl and gave them the middle finger as Suzie drove off. Aidan watched in the mirror as the girls returned to the shadows.

He wondered what else lurked there.

It was about ten minutes walk back from the Multiplex. Outside the protective box of the car, Aidan felt even more vulnerable, particularly when they stepped out of the bright lights of the cinema car park and into the streets that lay beyond. Again he was sure that every eye was on them.

It was a relief when they reached the pub and stepped inside.

The relief did not last long.

Although the jukebox was blasting out 'Don't look back in anger' at an ear assaulting level, it was obvious that they'd been seen and conversations had stopped. Self-consciously they walked up to the bar.

'What can I get you…officers?' said the barmaid.

'Just a coke for me,' said Suzie.

Aidan couldn't bring himself to order the same.

'Pint of bitter,' he muttered.

He paid and joined Suzie at a vacant table whose surface was sticky and ringed with more than tonight's drinks. The stool he sat on was dark with grease, he could almost feel the dirt grip his jeans and draw him onto the material like Velcro. The atmosphere was smoky overlaying the scents of stale beer, damp, and cheap perfume.

And still they were being watched. Some people were looking at them with downright hostility.

'Lovely place,' he murmured to Suzie.

She nodded. 'Yeah. It's worse than I remember.'

'So where is he?'

'How do I fucking know?'

The snap came as a surprise and not only to Aidan apparently. Suzie looked embarrassed. It hit him; she was on edge not just because of where they were but because she didn't know what she was doing either, she was just trying to do what her mentor Richard would have done. It should have been worrying but, actually, it was more reassuring.

'Richard said he was in here most days,' she said. 'That this was like his office.'

'We better wait then,' he said.

'Yup.'

He sipped his beer. No apology, he noted. That was at least in keeping with her character. By heck, she was abrasive and snappy.

There was a bleep from her phone. She picked it up and read the message.

'Is that him?' he said.

She looked up, right into his eyes.

'What?'

129

'Nothing. I was just wondering whether it was your contact texting you.'

She shook her head. 'Hardly. It's Sam. She worries about me.'

'Ah right, Sam.'

'What do you mean by that?'

Oh God. 'Nothing…er, is that him?'

A man had come into the pub and looked over at them.

She looked. 'Yes, that's Jimmy.'

He nodded. Relieved. Saved by the gangster.

Jimmy had gone over to talk to the landlord. He wasn't much to look at, certainly not in the mould of a TV crime boss. He had fair, rather unkempt and greasy hair retreating into a classic widow's peak, a pudgy face with a pasty complexion, an unhealthy pallor and paunch suggesting future - or perhaps current - cardiac problems. Amazingly he looked quite friendly, indeed he was the least threatening person Aidan had seen all night.

'Don't let that outside fool you,' Suzie whispered. 'Jimmy is into some pretty serious shit.'

She had leaned close to him. He found her breath on his ear quite disturbing.

Arousing.

This wasn't the time or place, he thought, and definitely not the right person to have such thoughts about.

'What do we do? Go over, introduce ourselves?'

'No. He'll decide. He knows who we are, well he knows who I am anyway, he should remember me.'

The conversation with the pub landlord was continuing. It was obvious that he and Suzie were the topic of conversation. Something struck Aidan; this wasn't a conversation of equals, the landlord was deferential, a minion reporting to a superior, waiting for orders.

At last a decision was reached. Jimmy nodded and headed to the bar. Rather than ordering though, he went through into it then headed upstairs, presumably to the living space above.

'What? What now?' said Aidan, confused.

'We wait,' said Suzie.

'But…'

The manager looked over to them and gave a little nod of his head towards the stairs.

Suzie got to her feet.

'Come on,' she said. 'We've been granted an audience with his majesty.'

Chapter Nineteen

May 8th 1997 8.40pm

Upstairs was, if anything, tackier and smellier than down.

Jimmy was in the kitchen, sat at the table. He looked at Suzie.

'I know you, don't I?' he said. 'You came to see me once with Richie boy?'

'That's right, I'm Suzie Regan.'

Jimmy nodded. 'Suzie, yeah. Forget names but not a nice bit of skirt.' He looked at Aidan. 'You, I don't know.'

'Aidan Hughes, I'm a reporter with-'

'I didn't say I wanted to know your fucking life story, kiddo,' Jimmy looked at Suzie. 'He with you? You can vouch for him? He's not a cop?'

'No, he's a reporter like me.'

Jimmy gave Suzie a grin. 'He ain't a bit like you, darlin'' he said, looking her up and down. 'Not from where I'm sitting.'

'How's business?' said Suzie.

'Ah, you know, not bad, considering.'

'Considering?'

'The economy's shit. 'Aven't you noticed?' Jimmy took out a tobacco pouch and rolled a cigarette. 'Times is hard.'

'I didn't think you'd be affected.'

''Course I am. People got less money to send my way.'

They were interrupted by the clink of glasses as the barmaid brought up a tray of drinks; two pints and a coke.

'Thanks, Nat,' said Jimmy running his fingers up the barmaid's leg and squeezing her behind as she leaned over to put the glasses down. 'When you goin' to let me show you what a real man can do?'

'When you divorce that bitch wife of yours,' said Nat.

Jimmy chuckled.

'Fair enough,' he said.

When she left Jimmy looked at Aidan.

'You don't say much, do you?' he said. 'You just window dressing?'

'I…er…' began Aidan but Suzie interrupted.

'We're a team,' she said. 'We're on a story.'

Jimmy leaned back and took a drink of his pint. 'What's that then? Blue badge forgeries? Old biddies being mugged?'

'Mickey Smith,' she said.

Jimmy demeanour changed instantly. The smile went and he put his glass down.

'What about him?' he muttered.

'We wanted to know what the word on the street was about what he was doing.'

Jimmy gave a snort of derision.

'The street? Mickey? He's gone legit, didn't you hear? He's a business big shot now.'

Aidan thought it was time to back Suzie up.

'Yeah, but we know that's not all he's involved in,' he said. 'He didn't give up his other interests, did he?'

Jimmy's look was withering. 'If you know what he's involved with, why you asking me about it?'

'Because your family's probably his biggest rival.'

Jimmy laughed.

'Yeah, right, we're major players, ain't we?' he said. 'We got Mickey quaking in his boots.'

'You wouldn't be upset if Mickey got taken down, would you?' said Aidan.

Jimmy looked at Aidan like he was a dog turd he'd just stood in.

'You're a fucking expert on that, are you?' he said. Jimmy stood and drained his pint, virtually pouring the beer down his throat. Aidan watched his Adam's apple bounce up and down with some fascination. He slammed the pint down on the table.

'You came here for information? I'll give you some fucking information - no not information, advice.' He pointed his finger at first Aidan and then Suzie. 'Drop it, both of you. Anything to do with Mickey Smith, forget it. Go back to reporting church fetes and missin' dogs cos you're out of your depth, both of you.'

Suzie's face was impassive. Aidan was impressed; she was not backing down.

'I didn't put you down as someone who was easily frightened,' she said.

'I'm not. You know me, I'm no angel.'

'Nope. And we didn't print anything about that, or mention you at all, last time, like we promised.'

Jimmy sat down and crossed his arms.

'So, you kept your word. Big deal.'

'Last time you were quite happy to talk about Mickey Smith, weren't you? In fact more than willing, you were eager.'

Jimmy shrugged.

'So?' he said.

'So what's changed?' said Suzie.

Aidan noticed one thing that had; Jimmy's attitude. He'd become less belligerent, quieter, more reflective.

'What's changed?' he said. 'Me, for one thing. I'm older and wiser - and still breathing. Then I was young, building my territory. I thought I could take the Smiths on. I thought you and Richie boy might be able to take him down. I know better now.'

'We might still-' began Aidan.

'No,' said Jimmy. 'No you can't, no one can. I mean, yeah, I'd have a fuckin' street party if he ever went, he's stamped on my fingers and stopped me doin' all sorts of stuff that I'd like to do, that I used to do, but it ain't going to happen. Nobodies goin' to help you either, not on this side of the fence.'

Suzie frowned. 'You said you weren't frightened.'

Jimmy shook his head. 'No, I said I weren't easily frightened. I'm scared shitless by Mickey Smith. It was bad enough a few years ago when I was gettin' goin' cos he was always hard and bloody ruthless, a wild young cannon. But now he's become something else.'

'Something else? What?'

'Unbeatable. Untouchable. People who go against him just… well, the best thing that happens to them is they die.' He looked straight at Suzie. 'Like your pal, Richard. He's dead. Yeah, I read the papers. And now I know he was looking into Mickey Smith, I know why. That's what happens now when you cross paths with him, that and worse. Mickey enjoys it, it's a game to him, fun.' Jimmy shook his head. 'He tolerates small fry like me because he knows we're shit scared of him, knows we ain't goin' to do anything. He likes that. If you've got any sense you'll walk away, find something else to make your name with.' He looked at Aidan now. 'Because if you carry on with this you're gonna fuckin' die.'

Chapter Twenty

May 8th 1997 10.20pm

'Here,' said Suzie, passing Aidan a massive gin and tonic.

He took the drink off her. It was more than welcome.

'So what now?' he said.

'We give up of course, what else?' Suzie slumped into one of her aunt's chairs and took a gulp of her own drink. 'Really, Aidan, what do you think we do? We find another way.'

'Yes, that's what I meant,' said Aidan, though he wondered whether he'd carry on if it wasn't for Suzie.

'I really thought Jimmy would help,' she said. 'He did last time, he had good reason to. I didn't expect he'd be like that.'

Aidan nodded.

'Are there any other contacts who do stuff for Mickey who might talk?'

Suzie shook her head. 'We couldn't get anyone who worked for him to talk last time, other than Hanif and you saw what happened to him.' She drained half her glass. 'There has to be a way. Richard obviously found something this time. We need his notes.'

'They've got them. He'd have kept them with him.'

'You don't think I fucking know that?'

'Don't talk to me like I'm a fucking moron!'

'Well if the cap fits…'

'Damn you, Suzie,' he said, getting up. 'A day working with you and I've had enough! You don't listen to me, you do nothing but order me about, and treat me and everything I say with contempt. You say we're in this together but we're not, not really. It's me that's been followed, me that's had to move out. Well, enough. Treat me with some fucking respect.'

He expected to get it all back, in spades.

Instead she stood up and held out her hand.

'At last,' she said. 'There he is.'

'Where who is?'

'The man I've been waiting to meet. The real Aidan Hughes. The one with a backbone, and anger and drive to do something. The one I can really work with.'

She still held her hand out.

'You really expect me to believe that, after what you said in the car?' he said.

'Oh come on, Aidan, I was angry with you then. Don't be like that.'

After a few moments Aidan gave in took her hand.

'Right,' she said. 'Can we get on now?'

Aidan nodded and sat back down as Suzie reached for the dossier.

* * *

May 8th 1997 11.15pm

Suzie sat back and sighed.

'Maybe the dossier isn't the way forward. It's all ancient history now,' she said.

'So if not that, what?'

'We should look at the accident again. That's what Richard started with. He found something.'

Aidan nodded. 'You're right but what do we do different? I talked to Rachel, the survivor. She changed her story.'

'Because you said someone got to her. The blond man. The same one you saw at the accident scene.'

'I think so, yes.'

'So he's the key. We need to find out more about him and how he fits into Mickey's organisation.'

'But how? We don't know his name, we don't know anything about him.'

'We do. We have an eyewitness. You.' She looked at him. 'So tell me what you saw.'

He stared at her confused. 'I have, I told you.'

'Not this way. Close your eyes, let your mind go blank and then think about it.'

'What?'

'Please, Aidan, humour me. It really works. Visualise either the accident or the hospital then give me your thoughts, your impressions.'

He sighed. 'Okay,' he said and closed his eyes.

'Take a few deep breaths as you're clearing your mind.'

He did.

At first he found it hard, his thoughts raced off in all directions, including along a diversion caused by Suzie's perfume, but at last he was able to visualise the accident and then the arrival of the blond man. What did he look like? Pale, thin, a pinched face, foreign looking.

Foreign.

'A Polish plumber,' he said, opening his eyes.

'What?'

'The man. That's the impression I got. Foreign anyway, not a native Brit.'

Suzie nodded thoughtfully. 'Interesting. Foreign and a plumber.'

'I could be wrong. It was just an impression.'

'Impressions are important. You saw him. He's probably foreign and he's not a heavy or someone professional like a lawyer.'

It was now Aidan's turn to nod thoughtfully. He had dismissed the exercise but it was actually useful. 'A blond, foreign non-entity who somehow fits into organised crime and can persuade the police to free a dangerous driver and a grieving widow to change her story and forget all about it. Who the hell can do that?'

'Exactly,' said Suzie. 'That's what we've got to find out. Where did he come from? Who is he?'

Aidan sighed. Maybe it hadn't got them that far after all. They still didn't know the important facts about him.

'How does someone like that survive in Mickey Smith's world?' said Suzie.

'Maybe he works at Urbania,' said Aidan. 'Wait, the Uni guys, the academics, one of those was foreign too. Gerhard Beck. He's East German. Well, just German now, I guess.'

'Interesting.'

'But he's not the blond man. I've seen a picture of him. He's short and plump.'

'Doesn't matter,' said Suzie frowning. 'East German, you definitely said East.'

'Yes, Dresden or Leipzig, somewhere like that. Why?'

'Because until 1990 that was in the Communist bloc. They did some weird stuff over there,' she said. 'Then the wall fell, the system collapsed, and the guys over there lost their backers.'

'So they looked to the West…Finch!' said Aidan. 'Mitchell Finch. He might have been the partner over here.'

Suzie nodded. 'Exactly. We need to find and talk to him.'

'It still doesn't explain how it links to Mickey Smith. It must be Urbania though. We need to know more about it.'

Suzie smiled. 'I think we're getting somewhere. Thanks to your memory. And there's a business link too, that's your area. You see, you are useful when you put your mind to it.'

The praise might have been faint and more than slightly condescending but it still made Aidan feel good.

Chapter Twenty-One

May 9th 1997 8.21am

The next morning saw Aidan sitting in the kitchen of his borrowed home, eating a bowl of cornflakes and musing over what to do next. Suzie, who'd slept over, had left late and was now in work.

Would he ever go back? Judging by the messages left by Gill virtually demanding his return, sick or not, or else suggested his days at the paper might be numbered. Unless he did something extraordinary.

Like bringing down Mickey Smith.

Something was niggling at Aidan. It was what Jimmy had said about the change in Mickey Smith, the point when he went from merely being a dangerous and ruthless operator to being invincible and unbeatable. He meant in the criminal world but it also applied to his property company, Urbania. It had come from nowhere, had no track record yet could do things that other companies couldn't; it could get the planning consents, it could sort out convoluted and seemingly insoluble legal issues and could obtain finance for the most speculative of schemes.

It was invincible and unbeatable.

And it had started to be that way at about the same time that Jimmy had said Mickey's crime enterprises had become the same. It had shown that with Maxwell Mill.

Four years ago.

When Richard was looking into them.

That seemed to be their first project. Maxwell Mill was

ground zero.

Suzie expected him to follow up on Finch and Beck and this wasn't technically doing that but surely this was related to what they did? He also remembered a lead, he knew someone who worked for the last developer to have the mill before Urbania, Nick Hollings.

It was years since they'd spoken, at least five in fact. Did he still have his number? He checked his contact book; yes he had one but what were the chances that it would still be right? Slim to none, he thought, Still he tried it.

It was answered on the third ring.

'Hello?'

The single word was delivered with many nuances. Aidan was ringing from his 'clean' mobile, Nick was being cautious answering a number he didn't recognise.

'Hi, Nick? It's Aidan. Aidan Hughes.'

'Aidan! How the devil are you? I thought you must have headed down to London.'

Aidan pulled a face. One of the main reasons he'd allowed his contacts to fade away was his embarrassment as others had progressed in their careers whilst his had stagnated.

'Nope, still around, still doing the same thing. How about you?'

'Getting by, you know. I went on my own a couple of years ago. The company's doing okay, even if I say so myself.'

'Great,' said Aidan, wondering how to move the conversation onto Maxwell Mill.

He didn't need to.

'Hey, this could work out well,' said Nick. 'I was just heading to the club, got a tee booked at ten fifty, it's the annual Manchester Developers Golf Day.'

'Oh, right.'

'You still write about property? I'm surprised I've not seen you at it before. It's the corporate event in the city.'

'Yes, I…' Aidan couldn't think of an explanation so mumbled something about always being too busy.

'Never mind, you're here for this one. Anyway, as I said, this could be handy. I've got a couple of investors invited and my partner's just cried off. Do you still play?'

Did he? He hadn't been on a golf course for three years.

'Yes,' he said. 'But I haven't got my clubs with me.'

'Not to worry, I can sort you out when we're there.'

'Fine then.'

'Right, I'll see you at the club. Oh, do you know where it is?'

Moments later Aidan was searching through Suzie's uncle's wardrobe, hoping that there was something suitable he could wear for the course. Jeans wouldn't cut it. Not at the most exclusive club in South Manchester.

Nick's 'doing okay' was obviously an understatement. Aidan felt even more left behind than ever.

He had to make this story work.

* * *

May 9th 1997 10.05am

'Aidan, what the hell are you wearing?'

He had expected Nick's reaction for, although Suzie's uncle was a golfer he was one who favoured Farah slacks and brightly coloured Pringle jumpers. He was also much taller than Aidan, hence everything was too long.

'It was all I could find at short notice where I'm staying.'

'Where you…? Oh forget it,' said Nick. 'I've got borrowed clubs for you but I think I'd better find you a top too. Don't want to scare the wildlife!' He smiled. 'Nor my clients.'

He followed Nick into the clubhouse and into the locker room.

'I've got a spare set in here,' he said. 'Here try this top for size.'

He reached into his locker and took the bag out and passed Aidan a pale blue jumper. As Aidan took his Pringle off and replaced it with Nick's top, another pair of golfers came in and started changing. 'Hey, Mickey, how's business?' Nick called over.

'Ah not bad, you know, Nicky boy, not bad.'

It took a few moments for the penny to drop who this was. Aidan thought he was going to be sick.

'Knowing you, Mickey that means pretty bloody good, eh?' said Nick. 'Do you know Aidan here, he's the property correspondent for-'

'Yeah, I know Mr Hughes. Let's just say our paths have crossed,' said Mickey Smith, smiling. 'I know all about him.'

Aidan couldn't speak. He just swallowed hard.

* * *

May 9th 1997 2.35pm

'That's three over, I'm afraid.'

'Bad luck, old chap.'

The handshakes on the 18th ended Aidan's ordeal which had seen him visit most quarters of the course during the round and lose half-a-dozen balls.

'Sorry, Nick,' he said as he shook hands with his partner. 'I was utter crap.'

'Hey, you haven't played for a while. And you did me a favour.' He pulled Aidan in closer and whispered. 'I think the money men feel sorry for me now so I might be getting a better deal.'

Aidan gave him a weak smile. As they walked towards the locker room he switched on his mobile. There were several texts and voicemails, all from Suzie, the gist of which was 'where the fuck are you?' and 'what are you doing on the story?'

The story. That was exactly why he was here. He'd almost forgotten.

'Is that work?'

'Sort of, yes.'

'You don't have to rush off, do you?' said Nick.

'No, I don't.'

In fact, he thought, it was essential he didn't. He needed something to justify the last four hours.

'Come and have a drink in the clubhouse then,' said Nick. 'I think you need it.'

Soon they were changed and in the bar. Sitting at a table near the balcony was Mickey Smith with his golf partners. He glanced across at Aidan and gave him that knowing, malevolent smile again.

'Here you go,' said Nick passing over a pint. He must have seen where Aidan was looking because he added; 'I didn't know you knew Mickey.'

Aidan had wondered how to shift the conversation onto this topic so this came as a Godsend.

'As Mickey said, our paths crossed once,' he muttered. 'His first development was Maxwell Mill, wasn't it? Didn't you have a go at that one too?'

Nick nodded. 'Well the developer I worked for then did, that was in my Burnt Umber days.'

'Burnt Umber?'

'The company was owned by an architect.'

'Ah. So what happened? Why did they sell out to Urbania?'

Nick pulled a face. 'You know, I don't know. It was a surprise. I mean, sure, we were struggling with it like everyone before had but our owner, Dennis, was determined to succeed. He was convinced that a design-led, eco project would win the planners and the conservation groups over.'

'Was it working?'

'Not really. Not enough anyway, we were haemorrhaging money but Dennis had become obsessed. He was going to get Maxwell Mill developed come hell, high water or bankruptcy.'

'But he sold?'

Aidan saw Nick glance over at Mickey Smith's table. Mickey was holding court. Nick's investors had gone over to shake his hand, to chat, they were respectful, deferential.

Power. Money. Influence. Mickey had it in spades.

'Yes, he did. It was strange. Dennis had just secured a new line of credit, it should have been enough to get us over the line with the consents and the compulsory purchase but then Mr Smith and his adviser rocked up at the office one afternoon. An hour later he'd sold it to them.'

'Did Dennis get a good price?'

Nick shook his head. 'We weren't supposed to know the terms but I had to prepare the figures for the annual report. Urbania paid about a quarter of what we paid for it eighteen months before.' Nick took a sip of his pint. 'Development values can and do change a lot but that was bloody crazy. It shafted the company. There was no way it could survive after that hit. That's why I went on my own; I had to. Still it worked out in the end.' Nick's gaze was still on Mickey Smith. It wasn't a friendly look.

'Did Dennis say why he sold?'

'Only that he said he realised it was the right think to do.' Nick chuckled. 'He kept repeating that: it was the right thing to do. We called it Dennis's mantra, that he only kept saying it because he needed to remind himself why he'd done it, that he didn't believe in why deep down.'

This was starting to sound familiar.

'A quarter,' Nick muttered. 'It really made no sense then nor now. Not after what happened with Maxwell.'

'They got their consents?'

Nick laughed. 'Of course they bloody did. It was like the pressure groups only stopped us because they hated our name. Urbania came along and all the objections vanished. Everything went; preserving this, rebuilding that, recasting all the ironwork in the original moulds, preserving the precious sightlines, it all went. They effectively got carte blanche. Then the council used their CPO powers and cleared all tenants out within three months and, to cap it all, they were rumoured to have got finance at some stupidly generous interest rate. No wonder they made a shitload of money.'

'How did they do all that?'

Nick stared at him incredulously. 'Do you think if I knew that I'd be here kowtowing to a couple of bankers begging for a few extra quid? No, I'd be on my private island counting my gold.'

'Urbania's that good?'

Nick nodded.

'They've done lots of other schemes haven't they? Since then? So their magic touch wasn't a one off?'

'Magic touch?' Nick gave a mirthless laugh. 'You could call it that. It's hard to get a look-in now on the best schemes. Us plebs are just left with the crumbs.' He looked across at Smith again. 'Or going begging to Urbania, cap in hand asking for a favour. Or a loan.'

'A loan? You've done business with Smith? You owe him money?'

'Had to,' Nick murmured. Abruptly he turned to Aidan. 'Wait, are you...?'

'Am I what?'

Nick's expression had changed. He drained his pint and stood up. 'I'm going to have to get back, mate. Said I'd be there for the kid's bath time.'

'What? Right, no problem. One last thing though, you said Mickey arrived with advisers. Who were they? Heavies?'

'Hardly. No, two foreign guys. Don't know why he bothered because neither spoke much English.'

Aidan swallowed. 'One blond and Polish looking, the other short, dark and plump?'

'Yes. How did you know?'

Before Aidan could reply his phone rang. It was Suzie.

'Where are you?'

'You're not supposed to take calls in here,' said Nick, looking towards the steward. 'It's against the rules.'

'Ring you back in five,' Aidan said before Suzie could speak, and rang off. 'Sorry.'

'That's all right.' Nick looked thoughtful. 'Can I have a word with you, before I go?'

'Sure, fire away.'

'Not here, outside.'

Puzzled, Aidan followed his friend out of the bar and outside into the car park.

'What is it?'

Nick glanced back at the clubhouse bar. 'All those questions about Smith. Are you doing a story on him?'

Aidan nodded. 'Yeah, I am.'

'Fucking hell! Is that why you contacted me out of the blue after all these years?'

'Well…'

'For fuck's sake, Aidan, really?'

'But Nick…'

'Don't but Nick me, you sodding arsehole.'

'What is it? What's the problem?'

'What's the problem?' Nick started walking towards his car. 'Oh, no problem, nothing at all. Oh, other than Mickey will now think I'm giving you the lowdown on him, that's all!'

'But you told me next to nothing!'

'Oh, I'm sorry about that, sorry that I'm not your Deep Throat.' Nick stopped, breathing heavily. 'For Christ's sake, man, I've got a wife and kid. Do you know what he's like?'

'I've got an idea…'

'So why did you do this? Let me guess, you found out he was a member here, knew I was too and engineered this?'

'No! You invited me, remember!'

'That was convenient...'

'I didn't bloody know Smith played here. Believe me, if I had I wouldn't have bloody well come.'

'Yeah, right.'

Nick stared at him, still breathing heavily, but at least the tirade had stopped.

'Don't come the innocent with me, you've done business with Smith haven't you? Well, haven't you?'

'Only because I had to,' Nick muttered. 'I'd rather have bloody not.'

'You still did. You still took money from him. Dirty money. Blood money.'

'Leave it, Aidan.'

'Why should I? Why should I take crap off you for doing a story on Mickey Smith when you've swum in the shit with him?' He put his hand on Nick's arm. 'Come on, help us take Smith down.'

Nick pushed him off. 'Take him down? You? Give me a break. You're a fucking moron.'

Before Aidan could stop him he walked the last few steps to his car.

'Sod off, Aidan,' he said. 'Don't call me again.'

He slammed the door and started the engine.

And then, in a shower of gravel, was gone.

Chapter Twenty-Two

May 9th 1997 4.09pm

Even before the gravel had settled, Aidan's phone was ringing again.

'What's going on? Where are you?'

He told her.

'A golf club? So I've taken the afternoon off to work on the story and you've pissed off to-'

'I'm working on the story not pissing around,' interrupted Aidan. 'Mickey Smith's here.'

'Oh, right. Smith's there? Fantastic! Have you got an interview?'

'An interview? Are you mad? This is a bloody gangster we're talking about here.'

'One who's supposed to be legit businessman. You're a business correspondent. It's a perfect excuse.'

Aidan was almost lost for words.

'To ask him what? "Excuse me, Mr Smith, did you kill Richard Tasker?"'

'Don't be stupid. Ask him about the crash, why he was allowed to walk away from a fatal accident.'

'But…'

'Actually, don't, I'll do it. I'm on my way. Oh, wait, have you got my car?'

'Yes I-'

'Right I'll take a taxi. Just keep him there.'

'How am I supposed to-'

But Suzie had rung off.

Keep him there? How exactly?

With no real idea he headed back to the bar. At least he could keep an eye on Smith over a pint.

But he immediately ran into a problem in the shape of one of the club stewards, smartly dressed in the clubs uniform, black trousers with a cream jacket, the club's crest on the breast picket.

'May I help you, sir?' he said.

'I just want a drink.'

'Are you a member, sir?'

'Well no but I was just in here…'

'Yes sir, I remember, with Mr Hollings, but I believe he's gone now.'

'Yes, he has.'

'Then I'm sorry, sir, We can't serve you. This is a members only club.'

'But…'

'Members and guests only, sir. Do you know any other members here.'

Aidan could not help but look over at Mickey Smith. He was in conversation with the others at his table but he had obviously seen Aidan's problems and was watching his confrontation with the steward with amusement.

'No,' said Aidan. 'I don't.'

'Then I will have to ask you to leave please, sir.'

Aidan just nodded, turned and walked out of the bar.

Now what?

He made his way into the entrance lobby. He had to stay here somehow, keep an eye on Smith, though how he was to stop him leaving was still beyond him. He could, at least, still see the bar from here and spent some time pretending to read the notices, which was full of handicap revisions, sign up sheets for competitions and the club committee minutes - nothing exactly riveting. There was a limit to how long he could hang about, the steward kept looking at him from the bar.

It was then he noticed he was still wearing the jumper Nick had lent him. He'd have to drop it off in the locker room and, whilst he was there, have a pee as he needed to go. He would lose sight of the bar but Smith showed no sign of leaving. He'd probably be all right for a few minutes.

Leaving Nick's jumper hung on the handle to his locker, he went to the gents adjoining the locker room.

There was no one in it and, with considerable relief, he stood at the urinal.

He was mid-flow when he heard someone come in behind him. He assumed it was another golfer coming to use the facilities. To his puzzlement he heard the door to the locker room being locked. Perhaps they closed it off after playing had finished but surely it was too early for that. There would still be players-

The blow was like nothing he'd ever felt before. The pain was instant and unbelievable, like his kidney had exploded. His knees buckled but before he could fall his head was thrust hard forward against the tiled wall impacting with a sharp crack.

Amidst his pain he felt a breath on his cheek.

'Do you really think you can take me on, you little shit?'

The voice was barely above a whisper but the menace was as clear as if delivered through a megaphone. 'Gave me the bird, didn't you? You in that stupid little toy car you must be so fucking proud of. And then you start poking your nose into my business, you and that other shit so-called reporter.'

Suzie? He knew about Suzie?

No. He was talking about Richard.

'I bet you thought you were so clever giving my boys the slip, didn't you? Well, didn't you?'

Smith drew back Aidan's head and then smashed it back into the tiles. He clearly wanted an answer.

'No, I-'

'Shut it, worm. Well let me tell you, Mr Hughes, this is my

town, understand? No one escapes me for long. So are you going to stop poking your nose into what doesn't concern you? Are you?'

He repeated the head smashing.

'Yes, yes I'll stop.'

Smith laughed. 'Yeah, of course you will. The thing is shithead, it's too late. You're a dead man, you just don't know it yet. It would have been easy to just have rubbed out, you know that? I'd just swat you like the blow-fly you are but that's too easy. I'm going to take my time with you. I'm going to dismantle you and your life, piece by piece. By the end you'll be begging me to put a bullet in your brain. And I'm going to enjoy it, believe me.'

His head was smashed against the tiles once more then the pressure on his body lifted as Smith let go. Aidan slumped to the floor, his chin cracking the urinal as he fell. He heard a laugh and footsteps walking away.

Smith had gone. For now.

He struggled to his feet, gasping for air. The pain in his kidney was not easing and his face was numb, his eye already closing, and his trousers were wet with urine. His hands were shaking so much that he could hardly turn the taps on to splash water on his face.

He heard voices from the locker room, laughter. Even if it wasn't Smith he couldn't be seen like this. He locked himself into one of the toilet cubicles, sat down and waited, hunched up, fighting the pain.

He had no idea how long he sat there, he'd lost track of time. When his phone rang it took a few moments to register, and longer still to force his still shaking fingers to press the right button.

'Yes?' he said.

'Where are you? Are you with Smith?'

'No, I'm...'

'What's with this place? They won't let me in because I've got jeans on and even then it would only be to the Lady Captain's bar? What fucking century are they existing in?'

'Are you in the car park?'

'Yes, why where are-'

'Stay there, I'm coming out.'

Aidan rang off. He stood up, unlocked the cubicle door and walked straight out of the gents, through the locker room and hallway and outside keeping his head down and without looking at anyone.

Suzie was near the doors.

'Where the hell...' she began then clearly saw the state he was in. 'What the...'

'Just get me out of here,' he said handing her car keys to her.

'But...'

'Please.'

'All right,' she said more quietly.

She had to help him into the passenger seat and put the seatbelt on him.

She had driven for around a minute before she asked the question he'd expected.

'What happened?'

He couldn't stop himself. He started crying.

Chapter Twenty-Three

May 9th 1997 6pm

'Are you alright in there?'

Aidan had his eyes closed, letting the shower's warmth ease his physical pains. He wished he could wash away his embarrassment so easily.

'Yes, I'm okay,' he said. 'I'm coming out.'

He turned off the water and, with some difficulty, stepped over the metal frame of the cubicle and put on the bathrobe that Suzie had found for him. He felt like he was ninety.

He limped out of the on-suite into the bedroom. Suzie was perched on the bed, her face troubled.

'We should get you to a doctor.'

'There's no need.'

'But…' she started then thought better of giving a sigh as a full stop. 'I've sorted you out some clean clothes. I went through your stuff. I hope that's okay?'

'Of course.'

'I'll let you get dressed.'

'Thanks.'

She got up and walked out of the bedroom.

Aidan immediately hit a snag. He struggled but eventually had to admit defeat. He closed his eyes. More embarrassment was on his way.

'Suzie,' he called. 'I can't bend to get my pants on.'

* * *

Later they sat in the lounge, both with a large brandy in hand.

'Sorry about that,' he muttered. 'And before, in the car. I don't know why I did that.'

'Forget it Aidan.'

'But I blubbed like a little girl.'

'Nah you didn't. Little girls are much braver than that.' She gave him a weak smile. 'Sorry, don't want to make light of it. It was natural, you were in shock.'

He nodded and took a sip of the fiery liquid, then shifted his position to ease the pain a little.

'Still the kidneys?'

He nodded.

'He did that with one punch?'

'Yup.'

'You really should go to hospital.'

'No,' he said. 'That would mean involving the police.'

'So? He assaulted you. This was a physical attack.'

Aidan stared at her in surprise. 'You've always been dead against involving them.'

'Yes, about the story, sure, but this is different. This is assault.'

Aidan took a deep breath, then winced at the pain that this caused. It made thinking difficult.

'There were no witnesses,' he said. 'Smith made sure of that. Even I didn't actually see him. All I've got is the bruises. It would be my word against his. I think we know who'd win.'

Suzie puffed out her cheeks. 'Yeah,' she said. 'I guess you're right.' She took a sip of her brandy. 'Do you want to stop?'

'What? No, no way.'

'But after he-'

'No, particularly after this I want to go on. I want to get the bastard more than ever.'

Suzie nodded. 'Good. I thought you would. I just wanted to hear it from you.' She frowned. 'But going after Smith directly isn't working. We need to be cleverer.'

He nodded. 'Yes. I think you're right. But what?'

'What about Smith's wife?'

'What do you mean?'

'She's not from a criminal background. She comes from money, her father's a stockbroker. She's in the Cheshire polo set.'

Now it was Aidan's turn to frown. 'You think she doesn't know what Mickey is? Really?'

Suzie shrugged. 'Maybe turns a blind eye. But if there's a threat to her lifestyle?'

He shook his head. 'I can't see it. Anyway, if Smith is twitchy about us poking about his business activities, what's he going to be like if we start sniffing about his family? He'd go ape-shit.'

'So what then?'

'What about Finch and that other guy, Beck? That was the original plan, to look at them.'

She pulled a face. 'Two academics. What the hell do they have to do with it all?'

'Exactly.'

'What do you mean?'

'I mean that's exactly what we need. A left-field approach to it all, something that Smith might ignore. The two aren't big-time crooks, they may know something. They may be the weak link we need.'

Suzie puffed out her cheeks, then looked at her watch.

'I'd better get back, Sam will be worried,' she said. 'I can't spend another night away, she's getting twitchy about it.'

'All right. But what about Finch and Beck?'

'I suppose you could look at them whilst I'm gone. If you want. Right, get a good night's sleep. I'll call you first thing.'

Later, after she'd gone, Aidan hit the brandy hard.

I suppose you could look at them. If you want.

Bitch.

He raised his glass. 'To you, Sam. Good luck to you,' he muttered.

Chapter Twenty-Four

May 10th 1997 8.40am

Aidan woke to a thumping head and a sore body. The memory of the nightmare that was the day before flooded back. His left eye was virtually closed. Seeking out a mirror confirmed his fears; he looked like he'd done a couple of rounds with Mike Tyson.

He was stuffed. Getting nowhere with the story except to have attracted the attention of a ruthless, vindictive, cruel gangster. Getting nowhere with Suzie too. She was impossible, moody, dismissive, sharp-tongued. God she was pretty though. If only…

'Don't be so stupid,' he said to himself and headed for a long shower.

After, and on his second strong coffee, he started to feel better.

This was his chance, he knew he was right. For once he was going to trust his judgement and go with it.

He picked up his mobile and punched in a number.

It rang and rang. He checked the time, well after nine, he should be in. He rang again. It was only then when realised why it wasn't being answered; it was a Saturday.

God, he was losing track of time.

With a sigh he settled down to write up his notes.

* * *

May 11th 1997 12.05pm

His mobile rang.

'Hello?'

'Hey, how are you?' Suzie, and he could hear music in the background.

'How do you think? Like I've been hit by a fucking train. Where are you? I've been waiting for you to come over so we can work out what to do next.'

'Ah, sorry, I couldn't. It was hockey yesterday and then I just had to spend some time with Sam. She's feeling neglected.'

'Fuck Sam,' Aidan muttered.

'What?'

'Nothing. Are you coming over?'

'No, we've got friends round for a barbie and - '

Aidan rang off.

* * *

May 12th 1997 7.45am

Aidan rarely looked forward to Monday mornings but this was the exception. It had almost been like waiting for Christmas Day when he was a kid, the weekend had been interminable. It was probably too early to call but there was a chance he'd be in early.

The long shot came off.

'Bryn Parry?'

'Bryn, it's Aidan.'

There was pause at the other end.

'Aidan. I have to say I'm a bit surprised to hear from you. What the hell have you got into? What have you got me into?'

'What happened?'

'After you left the other day I got a visit. A couple of gorillas in suits. Wanted to know what you wanted, warned me off seeing you again.'

'Ah. Sorry.'

'Sorry? Christ, Aidan, did you know that was going to happen?'

'Then, no. Now yes, which is why I'm calling rather than visiting.'

'Thanks for that. It wasn't pleasant. Luckily security came and escorted them off the premises. The university have been good too. I've got a sort of bodyguard keeping an eye on me twenty-four seven.'

'That's a relief. It's probably sensible too.'

There was a silence at the other end of the line.

'I hate bullies,' said Bryn. 'And I hate bastards trying to manipulate others.'

'I said I was sorry.'

'Not you. The people you're after. They're nasty pieces of work I guess?'

'Yes, they are. The worst.'

Another pause.

'Have you got a shot at bringing them down?'

Now Aidan hesitated.

'I don't know,' he said deciding on honesty. 'Maybe. It's not looking great at the moment.'

'Would knowing more about Beck and Finch help?'

'I think so, yes.'

'Right then. What I know is little more than rumours, that's why I didn't want to repeat them but, sod it, if it helps, you might as well hear them from me.

'The reason why Finch and Beck were dismissed was down to Beck's research. It came to light that he'd done lots of weird stuff back in East Germany sponsored by the Stasi.'

'Weird stuff? What like?'

'Human experimentation. Deep brain surgery based on some mumbo-jumbo crap involving parapsychology and behaviour modification.'

'Jesus.'

'Exactly. Apparently he brought some of that research with him to Manchester, including, though this really is absolutely a rumour, some of his subjects, the poor bastards. The ones that survived at least. One of the chaps in medical research I talked to who was on the disciplinary committee who decided on the sackings said that nineteen out of twenty people who went through that sort of procedure would end up as a vegetable. Not surprisingly the university couldn't be associated with anything like that. Finch was in cahoots with Beck so he had to go too.'

Aidan immediately thought of the blond man. Was he one of Beck's subjects?

'Wow,' he whispered.

'Yup. Deep shit, huh? Does it help?'

'I think so, yes.'

'Good. Oh, although I've no idea where Beck is, Finch had a visiting lectureship at the Business School at Salford. He may well still have it. I know Finch, in business or not, being an academic was important to him. He'd want to keep that post.'

'That's brilliant, Bryn, thanks.'

'No problem. Well, I say that but…'

'Keep my distance until this is sorted?'

Bryn laughed. 'Nothing personal,' he said. 'I'd just like to keep my boyish good looks intact.'

'Understood Bryn.'

'Good luck with your sleuthing.'

'Cheers.'

As soon as the call ended Aidan gave a fist pump 'Yes!' he said.

He opened up Netscape and called up the university's homepage. Sure enough, Finch was listed as a visiting academic.

He sat back, thinking. The universities would be coming to

the end of term, exams would start at the end of the month and continue into June but lectures and tutorials would still be happening. It was coming up to 8.15 am, perhaps a bit early to call to see if Finch was teaching. He'd give it a few minutes.

To pass the time he did another search on behavioural and brain research carried out behind the Iron Curtain. He didn't expect too much but found more than he expected, even if much of the sources seemed based on hearsay rather than hard evidence. If the gossip was accurate, much of the research seemed to smack of medieval superstition rather than hard science but, in a totalitarian state looking to maintain control over it's people, nothing appeared to be off-limits. Still some of the procedures reported were brutal, reminding him of Josef Mengele's research in the death camps.

Should he be surprised though? The west had brushed a lot of stuff under the carpet to get hold of things like German rocket research. He thought of the quote attributed to Werner Von Braun; 'I aimed at the stars but sometimes I hit England…' and smiled to himself. Yes, just because research came from the most heinous of sources didn't mean that it wouldn't be used and built on. He wouldn't be surprised if research on the brain and behaviour would follow the trends of rocket science.

And it would be much easier to keep secret.

But mind control? Science fiction. He'd like to see himself trying to run that one past Suzie.

He bit his lip thoughtfully. It was now after half-past eight.

Time to give the university a call.

But before he could he heard the key in the door.

'Only me,' Suzie called. 'Are you decent?'

'In the kitchen.'

'I took the day off as…bloody hell, that's a shiner.'

'Thanks. Not a pretty sight is it?'

'No. How are you feeling?'

'Sore. In more ways than one.'

She pulled a face. 'With me? Over this weekend?'

'Forget it, it's past history now. Coffee?'

'Please.' She smiled. 'No second thoughts then? You're still determined to see this through?'

'Lots of second thoughts but, yes I want to get the bastard. And I think I've got a lead.' He told her about the conversation with Bryn.

She puffed out her cheeks. 'Finch and Beck again?'

'Yes. They're the key. I know it.'

'Come on, Aidan. You're surely not suggesting some weird East German research is behind this? I thought you were more sensible than that.'

'I think it's worth looking at,' he said.

'It's just a sideshow. I think we should-'

'No,' said Aidan. 'We're going to follow up on it. This is our best bet.'

He saw her start to object, then glance at his battered face. 'OK,' she said. 'I do owe you one after deserting you for 48 hours. Let's do it.'

'After another coffee,' he said.

As he made it he smiled. A win was a win, however it had come.

Chapter Twenty-Five

May 12th 1997 10.14am

'What time is it?'

'About ten-fifteen.'

'What time do academics start?'

'When they feel like it probably.'

Suzie puffed out her cheeks.

'How would they survive in the real world?' she muttered.

'Here they don't need to worry about reality all that much,' said Aidan.

They'd arrived just before nine, based upon Finch's department confirming that they did expect him in 'sometime today', joining the streams of students heading into the Maxwell building. There were big queues at both the newsagent and the cafe at first but these eased off after nine as people headed off to lectures. The lounge further back then filled with students and staff drifting in and out as their morning commenced, with another rush just before ten as the next round of lectures started but had eased off again straight after.

There had been no sign of Finch despite his department telling them he had a seminar later and appointments with students before.

They had positioned themselves at a table which gave a good view of both the main entrance and the stairs that led from the middle of the building to the lecture rooms and offices above. It was unlikely that they'd have missed him but Suzie had gone up to check whether he was in his department a couple of times. Whilst she had, he noticed a few people glance at his swollen face then look away. He really must look a sight.

Whatever, they were drawing a blank.

A group of lads wearing university rowing club t-shirts took a table near them, all over six foot, muscular with stomachs annoyingly flat. Was he ever that fit? Well the first few years of work life would bring them back to earth.

'I should have come to uni here,' murmured Suzie, who had obviously also seen them.

'I thought you should be ogling the girls,' said Aidan.

'Just because Sam and I have a thing doesn't mean I don't swing both ways, Aidan. I like cock too. Grow up, this is 1997 not 1957.'

'Yes, of course, sorry.'

So she and Sam definitely were…

'That's Finch isn't it?'

He looked across to the newsagent where a tall man with a mane of greying hair was buying a paper.

'Yes, that's him.'

'What's the plan? Wait until he goes upstairs and then corner him?'

Aidan didn't answer. He was watching Finch. He looked nervous and had stopped to scan the lounge.

'What's he doing?'

'He's looking for someone,' said Suzie.

She was right. He'd paused, pretending to read his paper but he was obviously scouting out the room. Then his gaze fell on Aidan and Suzie and he stopped.

'Shit, he's looking for us, someone's warned him.'

'But how…? Oh, sod it, they must have bugged Bryn's phone.'

Finch turned on his heel and walked back towards the entrance.

'He's off again.'

They hurried after him, hindered by the mass of students milling around the entrance foyer.

'Where is he? I've lost him.'

'There!' Suzie pointed. 'Crossing the road.'

She started to run. Aidan jogged after her. Finch was on the median strip of the four-lane road, waiting for a gap in the traffic or for the lights to change, which they now did, allowing him to reach the far side. The pelican crossing's light flashed to orange and the cars started to move as Suzie reached the road but she didn't hesitate; she crossed, making a Ford driver stand on his brakes. Aidan followed, ignoring the blaring horns and the drivers' curses as Suzie, younger and far fitter, left him behind.

'Dr Finch, Dr Finch!' he heard her shout. 'Don't be stupid, you can't run forever.'

They'd gone out of sight down a side street. Aidan was puffing hard now; he really would have to go on a diet, get to the gym. Turning the corner, he was pleased to see Suzie had run down their quarry. He panted up to them.

'You'll have to talk to us sometime,' said Suzie.

'I don't have to talk to anyone I don't want to, now get out of my way!'

Suzie was doing her best line-backer impression, stepping in front of Finch, blocking him.

'It would be better for everyone if you did talk.'

'Better? How? Get out of my way. I'll call the police!'

'Will you? What would Mickey Smith say about that?'

Finch seemed to flinch at the name. 'Mickey Smith? I don't know anyone called Mickey.'

'Oh yes, right, of course you don't. I'm sure this university would be very interested in who you're associated with. Your last employers were, weren't they? Do Salford know why you were asked to leave your post at UMIST, why you had to give up your tenure?'

'Why would they listen to the likes of you? I don't even know who you are.'

'Rubbish, you know who we are, that's why you ran,' sighed Suzie. 'But we'll play along with this stupid charade. Here's my card.'

She held it out and Finch took it without looking. Aidan did the same, aware that the mobile number on it was his old one, the one he'd stopped using because of the hack.

'Come on, Dr Finch,' he said, able to speak at last. 'Suzie's right. This isn't something we're going to drop, we'll publish anyway. It'd be much better for you if you gave us your side of the story.'

Finch stopped trying to dodge past Suzie. 'Publish? What are you going to publish? They said you had nothing.'

'Well Mickey Smith would say that, wouldn't he?' said Suzie. 'He's running scared. We've got the lot.'

Aidan had to admire her front; he almost believed her.

And it was clear that Smith wasn't the only one running scared.

'Oh my God, my God, no!' said Finch. 'I knew it would come out, I just knew it!'

'Well it has, so come on, tell us your side whilst you still can. If you don't talk now it will be too late, it will all be out there.'

Finch was breathing hard, harder even than Aidan had been after his recent exertions, and sweating profusely, his eyes bulging. 'I can't be seen with you, I just can't! They'll be watching me.'

Abruptly he tried to break away, pushing Suzie so hard she stumbled and fell. Aidan acted instinctively, grabbing Finch and pushing him up against the wall.

'Don't you want to stop all this?' he found himself saying. 'Wouldn't you like your life to go back to what it was before you got involved with Smith?' He saw Finch look at Aidan's swollen face. 'Yes, this is Smith's handiwork. This is what he can do. But you can make it all go away.'

Suzie had recovered.

'Don't you wish that would happen, Dr Finch? That things would go back to how it was before you got involved with Smith?'

Finch stopped struggling. 'Yes,' he whispered. 'I do. Every day.'

'We can do that. We can make it happen. We can protect you.'

How are we going to do that, Aidan thought, but said nothing.

'Protect me…' Finch murmured.

'Yes,' said Suzie. 'You just need to talk to us. Confirm what we know. We'll print the truth.'

'But I can't, he'll see-'

'No, he won't. Look around you, there's no-one here. There's nobody to see.'

Finch scanned the street around him.

'Then you don't know him,' he said. 'He's everywhere. He knows where I go, what I do, what I think. He knows I was coming here today. He'll send people.'

'Then let's drive somewhere, out into the country, where it's quiet. Somewhere where we can spot someone coming a mile away. How does that sound?'

Her tone was honey sweet, persuasive. How could anyone resist this, Aidan thought? Even in the moment he was jealous of her skills. It was an invaluable skill for a reporter, one he didn't have.

It was a weapon. And it worked.

Finch had fallen under the spell.

'Yes,' he nodded. 'Yes, it sounds good.'

Suzie nodded towards the car park. 'Is your car in there?'

'Yes.'

'Let's go then, quickly before anyone sees us.'

Finch led them to his car. Aidan was impressed. It was a top of the range BMW 7-series, one with the V12 engine, less than a year old by the reg plate.

Not exactly a typical academics car.

Finch unlocked it with a blip of a remote and they got inside, Aidan in the back, Suzie in the passenger seat.

'Where should we go?' he said.

'Up to you,' she said. 'Wherever you feel safe. We're in your hands.'

He nodded and started the engine, the twelve cylinders burbling into life.

'All right,' he muttered and drove out of the car park and left onto Salford Crescent.

Despite the climate control working to cool the interior, Finch was sweating profusely. Aidan could see him continuously checking the mirror, so much so that Aidan himself looked over his shoulder at the traffic behind. There were other cars but whether any of them was following was impossible to tell.

Finch clearly felt the same.

'What am I doing?' he said. 'This is madness, you should-'

'Great car, this,' Aidan jumped in. 'It's the V8 version isn't it?'

'No, it's the twelve,' said Finch.

'Ah right, good choice,' said Aidan, seeing Suzie turn and gave him a puzzled look. 'Is it an auto?'

'Yes, that's right.'

He winked at Suzie and she gave the slightest nod of understanding -and approval - as to what he was doing.

Distraction.

Diversion.

'Never driven an auto but it must suit the V12.'

'It does. It's a great drive.'

'Love to try it.'

'Are you into cars?'

'I've got an Alfa Spyder. Bit different from this, very old school.'

'Yes. I love the gadgets in this though.'

Aidan nodded and glanced out of the window. Good, they were well out of town now and Finch was much calmer. Suzie glanced at Finch and then back at Aidan and gave that little nod again. It's meaning was clear; well done.

He could live with that.

'Where are you thinking of going?' said Suzie.

'I don't know. A pub?' said Finch.

'It's a bit early for that. Bent's garden centre is down this way, isn't it?'

'Yes, it is.'

'It's got a coffee shop. It shouldn't be too busy at this time of day. Left at this roundabout.'

'A garden centre on a weekday morning will be full of pensioners,' Finch murmured, but did as Suzie suggested.

Finch was right. Bent's car park was already half full and, when they made their way through to the coffee shop, it was apparent where most of the occupants were.

They found a table in one of the few quiet corners and Aidan went and bought a pot of tea for three. When he came back, Finch and Suzie were talking quietly; he guessed that Suzie was keeping off topic but was making small talk. Finch had recovered some of his poise but his eyes still darted nervously this way and that.

Aidan poured the tea.

'Now,' said Suzie. 'Shall we start?'

Chapter Twenty-Six

May 12th 1997 11.45am

'Thanks for agreeing to talk to us.'

Finch gave a derisive snort. 'You haven't exactly given me much of a choice, have you?'

'You do have a choice. You can just walk away. But-' Finch started to rise. ' - it would be a mistake.'

'Why?'

Suzie looked at him earnestly. 'Because you've got yourself involved with one of the biggest criminals in Manchester, a man who deals in drugs, peddles the bodies of young women, earns money from extortion and fear, who orders murders like he was ordering a takeaway. That's the man you've associated with. That's the man who's going to taint your reputation.'

Finch sat down again.

'I don't know anything about that. Smith is a businessman. He works in property development. He has casinos.'

'Keep telling yourself that, Dr Finch.'

'It's true…'

'You may have thought that at the start, when you and Beck first went to him but you've found out different since, haven't you?' said Aidan.

'You unlocked the tiger's cage and let it out, didn't you? You thought it was your ticket to wealth and power. But now the beast is out you can't control it. All you can do now is keep quiet and try not to get eaten,' said Suzie. 'That's right, isn't it, Dr Finch?'

Finch didn't speak. He just nodded.

'So why did you sell your soul to the devil?'

'It wasn't like that,' Finch muttered.

'Why don't you tell us how it was?' Suzie took out her Dictaphone and placed it on the table.

'I'm not talking with that on,' Finch pointed at it. 'Put it away or I walk.'

Aidan reached over and picked it up, putting it in his shirt pocket, making sure that the red light showing it was recording was up against his body. 'There, it's gone,' he said.

He saw Suzie give a brief smile, then start at Finch again.

'Come on. Tell us. Get it off your chest.'

Still Finch hesitated so Aidan decided to use what he knew about academics as leverage.

'It was all Beck's idea, wasn't it? He wanted to find someone to use his research.'

This had the required effect. Finch looked affronted.

'Beck had no idea what he had,' he said. 'Yes, he'd done the basic research but he didn't have the vision as to how to use it. It was me that saw the opportunity. It's where I've made my name; lateral, creative thinking, seeing business opportunities for blue sky research. Gerhard is a typical scientist, good in his field but very limited in his vision.'

Suzie nodded. 'You see, that's why we need to hear your side of things, to get the story straight.'

'Yes, I see.'

'So going to Smith was your idea?'

Finch suddenly seemed to realise the hole he'd just dug for himself. 'Yes but…I…I…didn't know what he was involved with, how he'd use it. I'm innocent of that. I didn't know. I was just the facilitator.'

'Eichmann,' Aidan muttered under his breath.

'What?' said Finch.

'Nothing,' said Aidan.

'We can show your innocence when we publish,' said Suzie.

'But we can only do that if you tell us everything.'

Finch nodded.

'Alright,' he said. 'I first met Gerhard when he came to Manchester five years ago. He'd accepted a position as a research assistant in psychology and his department was making a joint bid to the ESRC for a research grant with mine.'

'ESRC?' said Suzie.

'The Economic and Social Research Council of course,' snapped Finch. 'God, you people are ignorant.'

'A research assistant,' said Aidan, trying to get Finch back on course. 'That's quite a lowly position isn't it? I thought Beck-'

'Professor Beck was a senior academic in Germany. He had nearly thirty years experience. It was an absolute disgrace that he was forced into taking something like that.'

'An academic in East Germany,' said Suzie.

'Yes, East Germany. You make it sound like a crime. People can't help where they're from. And the eastern bloc universities did some excellent work. They couldn't help the system they did it in.'

'Some of the work they did was a crime though, wasn't it?' said Suzie.

'Possibly,' muttered Finch. 'With hindsight.'

'So why did Beck, sorry, Professor Beck, lose his position after reunification?'

Finch paused, clearly choosing his words carefully.

'His research was government funded. That funding was not renewed when the West...' his voice trailed away.

'Was that because it involved-' began Suzie but Aidan interrupted, flashing a warning glance at her.

'So Professor Beck came to Manchester,' he said. 'To find work?'

'Yes, he did. And this wasn't the first place he came. Poor Gerhard had to live hand-to-mouth, moving from place to place, accepting pittances just to survive. A total disgrace. He should not have been in that position. His experience and skills were just not recognised as they should have been.'

'You must have seen a kindred spirit in him,' said Aidan.

'What do you mean by that?' said Finch, frowning.

'I meant that some people find it difficult for their abilities to be recognised in a university. It's a dog-eat-dog world isn't it?'

'You could say that,' muttered Finch. 'Have you worked in one?'

'He knows Bryn Parry,' said Suzie.

Finch gave her a hard stare. 'Well, there's a case in point. Promoted beyond his true abilities because he's good looking and performs well in front of the cameras. Hard graft and good practice is totally overlooked. It's all about that these days. Like this bounder Blair. He's not a socialist. It's all PR.'

Aidan nodded. He didn't have to pretend to agree because he agreed with everything Finch had just said. Particularly about Bryn. It was clear Finch was as jealous and frustrated as he was. But that wasn't helping anyone. Things needed to move on.

'You're right,' he said. 'And I guess you had personal experience of your work not being fully recognised?'

Finch snorted. 'Thirty-five published papers, two research grants and still I get passed over for promotion. It wasn't fair.'

'So when Beck came along and told you about his research you saw a chance to put that right?' said Suzie.

'Yes! The people getting promotions and reaping the rewards from their work were all in real-world technology and knowledge transfer - start-up businesses. I've written papers on it. I had one in Forbes, it was well-received and cited, stressing the-'

'So you saw an opportunity with Professor Beck's previous work,' said Suzie quickly.

'Yes, when he outlined what The Mule could do it was clear that the possibilities were endless. Businesses would fall over themselves to exploit his abilities.'

There was a pregnant silence with neither he nor Suzie having a question ready to fill it. He guessed that she was the same as him, thrown by the reference. The Mule? What was a mule? A mule was a courier wasn't it? He'd heard of drug mules, surely he wasn't one of those. But who or what was he?

Finch was frowning, looking at each of them in turn. Shit, if one of them didn't say anything he'd guess how little they actually knew and then he'd be gone.

Luckily Suzie recovered.

'Yes, that fits in with what we've heard,' she said, tapping her pen on her notebook. 'So that was when you set up Astcanza?'

'Yes, of course,' said Finch. 'We had to move quickly before anyone else did.'

'But setting up Astcanza led to your dismissal? Was that because of your associating with Smith?'

'I was not dismissed!' said Finch. 'I resigned. And that had nothing to do with Smith and Urbania.'

'So what was the cause?'

'It was unacceptable interference from the university. They were unhappy with Gerhard's involvement. They wanted him removed as a director. And then they sacked him from his position. Mental pygmies. Luddites.'

'They were partners in the company? They provided seed investment?' said Aidan.

'Unfortunately, yes.'

'So Beck's previous research activities, including his experiments, came out?' said Suzie.

'What do you mean by that?'

'Did you see any of the poor sods Beck turned into vegetables with the surgery he carried out on them?'

Finch was on his feet. 'I don't have to listen to this,' he said. 'This interview is over.'

'You can leave if you want,' said Suzie. 'But that would mean we print what we have, warts and all, and put your name against it. Your university wouldn't like that, would it? You'd lose that post too.'

Finch glared at her but sat down again.

'You don't have anything on me,' he muttered.

'Really?' said Suzie. 'Is that why you're shit-scared of what we'll print?'

Finch's discomfort seemed to be the perfect opportunity to put the key question; 'So how did you get involved with Smith?' said Aidan.

'I'd met him about a year before. He was setting up Urbania and attended one of my business seminars. He was frustrated, clearly a man who was used to getting his own way; that wasn't happening in the business world and it annoyed him.'

'So when you set up Astcanza with Beck, you saw him as a way to make money?'

'Money wasn't everything,' said Finch. 'The key thing was proof of concept, to show that Beck's research worked in the real world.'

'Which it did?'

Finch nodded. 'Very well.'

'So well, in fact, that Mickey Smith wanted exclusivity?'

Finch nodded again.

'Did you accept it?'

'Not at first,' whispered Finch.

'But then the university pulled Astcanza's funding?'

'Yes.'

'So you went to Smith for the cash?'

Finch nodded.

'He wanted to buy you out?'

'At first, yes. There was some money exchanged. Then the offer changed.'

'To simple survival?' said Aidan.

Once again Finch nodded.

'Did he offer the same to Beck?'

Now the nod was so slight as to be almost non-existent.

'Did he accept?'

A shake of the head.

'Is Beck still alive?' said Suzie.

Another shake.

'We've not seen an obituary.'

Finch laughed. 'Surely you know the way Smith operates?' he said.

'Did the Mule kill him?'

'What?'

'Well that's what he is isn't he, a hit man, trained to be ruthless, to have no enmity. That's what the surgery was about wasn't it?'

Finch looked bewildered. 'A hit man?' he murmured. He stood up. 'You don't actually know anything, do you? You're fishing. Bloody hell and I fell for it.'

Before they could stop him, Finch was up, pushing the table over then strode swiftly toward the entrance.

Chapter Twenty-Seven

Finch had caught them on the hop and also had luck on his side as a coach full of pensioners had just pulled up outside the entrance, its passengers streaming off. He darted through the door before they started to come through it. By the time Suzie and Aidan got there they were confronted by a near solid grey wall.

'Fuck it!' said Suzie loudly.

'Language, young lady,' said one of the pensioners.

'Some people should learn their manners,' said her companion. 'Wait your turn, we were here first.'

Suzie gave her a dark look and fumed quietly as the rest of the party, at least thirty in number, ambled unhurriedly through the door, chatting noisily. Some smiled at Aidan and Suzie.

Suzie scowled back at them.

'He'll be long gone,' she muttered. 'We've lost him. And we're stranded here. We'll have to get a taxi back.'

'Wait…his car's still here,' said Aidan, pointing.

'What? Yeah you're right. Yes, love it is a lovely day, take your bloody time,' she said as, at last, the final pair in the coach party were inside.

Aidan followed her into the car park.

'So where's he gone?' she said.

'I dunno…there!'

Aidan had spotted Finch. He was on the far side of the vast car park, stood behind a car, one hand resting on the boot, in the other was his mobile, he was speaking into it. Even from a few hundred yards away, he could see Finch was breathing heavily, and the reason why was clear; three men were closing in on him. Finch was cornered.

'Fuck, they're going to whack him,' said Suzie. 'He must be calling for help.'

She started towards them but, to Aidan's relief, stopped. The last thing he wanted to do was blunder into a gangland killing. The assassins were unlikely to take the intrusion well.

'Surely not in broad daylight, in public,' she said.

Finch tried to run but two of the men caught him by the arms, holding him still. The third, smaller man closed in.

Small. Lightly built. Blond.

'It's not a hit,' said Aidan and started to run towards the men. 'Hey!' he shouted.

It all seemed to happen in slow motion. Finch leaning away from the blond man, looking terrified. Then the heavies released him, the three walking swiftly away.

Finch's body language had abruptly changed. He was suddenly relaxed, the fear had gone. Aidan reached him, Suzie just behind.

'Dr Finch,' he said. 'Are you okay?'

Finch didn't show any sign of recognition, or, indeed, any sign that he'd seen or heard the reporters. He just walked right past them, his eyes glassy, face blank.

'What the fuck?' said Suzie.

'I know,' said Aidan.

'What…?'

'That was him. That was the blond man.' He thought about what Finch had just said. 'That was the Mule.'

'The Mule?'

Finch had reached his car.

'We should stop him,' said Suzie.

'There's no point,' said Aidan. 'I've seen this before. He won't know us. He'll have forgotten everything.'

'But…'

Finch started his car, put it into drive, pulled out of the car space and floored the throttle.

'What the…'

It was perhaps one hundred yards to the car park entrance, by which time the big saloon was doing at least fifty mph.

Aidan saw people throwing themselves out of the way. There was a scream, then the car crossed the road, leaped into the air as it struck the kerb on the far side, landed and, still accelerating, crossed the pub car park on the far side and plunged beneath the trailer of an articulated lorry parked up in the far corner. The BMWs roof was stripped off.

Chapter Twenty-Eight

May 12th 1997 12.41pm

'Shit!' said Suzie and started running. Aidan followed but, again, had no chance of keeping up with his super fit colleague. She had already crossed the road as Aidan reached the entrance to the garden centre. He was about to follow when he noticed a couple sprawled on the pavement, she bleeding from the knees where she had fallen, him staggering to his feet.

'Polly! My poor little Polly!' wailed the woman. 'Where is she?'

For a moment he thought she was asking about another person - a child? - and he looked around, afraid of what he might see. Then he saw the dog, or what had been a dog, whose body had been flung across the carriageway by the BMW.

The traffic had already stopped, motorists were out of their cars and looking towards the crashed car, so it was safe for Aidan to cross. The dog was small, white and fluffy; he couldn't tell the breed and it was most definitely dead.

'Polly! Polly! No, no!'

Aidan turned and stopped the woman getting closer.

'No, love,' he said. 'You'd better not. I'll deal with her.' He looked at the crowd who'd gathered. 'Could someone take this lady inside? She needs treatment.'

As he spoke, and as people hurried over to hustle the woman away, he saw something; the blond man.

He was stood by a car, the rear passenger door open, engine running. He was staring at Aidan - no, not at Aidan, at the body of the dog. It was the look on his face that was so striking. Previously, each time Aidan had caught fleeting glances of him, his face had been bland, impassive, showing no emotion. Now he was showing it; he was distraught, anguished.

One of his minders got out and forced him into the car. The blond man resisted, his eyes fixed on the broken little body but he was forced inside. Moments later, the car was moving, picking its way carefully and unobtrusively through the rubberneckers and towards the proper exit, a few hundred yards back up the road towards Warrington. It soon vanished from Aidan's sight.

Suzie reappeared.

'He's dead,' she said. 'The impact took the top of his head off. It's not a pretty sight. Oh fuck...' she added, looking down at the dog.

'Yep,' sighed Aidan. 'I'll need to deal with this first. But you wouldn't believe what I just saw.'

Chapter Twenty-Nine

May 12th 1997 2.05pm

It took thirty minutes for the taxi to arrive, during which time they made themselves scarce. They had no desire to talk to the police so walked down to the roundabout on the East Lancs road to be picked up there. Other than Aidan describing to Suzie what he'd seen, they hardly said a word to each other. It was the same in the taxi, then in the car journey from Salford back to Suzie's aunt's home.

Only then did Suzie sum up their day.

'Fuck.'

It was succinct, but accurate.

'Yeah,' he said.

'Why did he do that?' she said. 'He was in control all the way to the impact. His foot was still on the accelerator. I had to turn off the engine.'

'It was deliberate.'

'But why kill himself? He was confident, arrogant even, when he walked out on us. He knew we had nothing substantial on him, he'd worked out we were just fishing.'

'Yup.'

'But then, two minutes later, he drives his car under a Tesco lorry and splatters his brains all over the landscape. Why?'

'Simple; he talked to the blond man.'

She shook her head. 'Not that again. It can't be.'

'You saw with your own eyes. He's the Mule.'

'But…yes, he could be but what actually is a Mule?'

'He's-'

'He could be just a messenger. A mule can carry things, can't they?'

'But that's not what we-'

'Yes, the Mule delivered a message,' Suzie was now in full flow. 'It had to be a threat, from Smith.

'A threat? Really? That explains all that does it?'

'Yup. That man is Mickey Smith's consigliere. He has to be.'

He stared at her in disbelief.

'Him? Really? You saw him? What did he look like to you, someone who could even survive in Mickey Smith's world, let alone rise to be Smith's right-hand man?'

Suzie shook her head.

'Okay, you're right on that. He looked like you said; like a Polish plumber.' She screwed up her face. 'But what else could he be? Looks can be deceiving, can't they?'

'But-'

'Think of all those serial killers when everyone said "ooh, who'd have thought it? He looked so harmless."'

'No, you're wrong. He's a weapon. He's-' began Aidan but Suzie's phone rang.

She looked at the screen.

'Shit, it's Sam, I've got to take this.'

She walked out of the room and into the hallway.

Aidan shook his head. She wasn't listening to him, even after all they'd been through she was still dismissive of his opinions. Even after she'd witnessed the blond man - the Mule - in action, still she didn't believe it.

He plugged his laptop into the phone line and waited whilst it connected to the arthritic dial-up connection. After much clicking and whirring the machine brought up the Netscape home page, he then called up Excite to search.

He entered 'Mule' into the search box.

It brought up references to horse and donkey hybrids and, further down, to drug mules. He scrolled through the first three pages; more of the same.

But then Finch had said THE mule. Not A mule, not mule alone but The Mule, like it was a title - and one that he seemed to think they would get. And the annoying thing was it did ring a bell with him, albeit a faint and frustratingly elusive one.

He typed "The Mule" into the search box.

Suzie came back into the room, her phone pressed to her ear, before the dial-up had even filled the first page of results.

'Yes, yes, I will. This evening, I promise... Look I can't help it, there's a lot going on. No you've got nothing to worry about on that score. Right, well it's the truth. Look, must go...yes...yes... he's here but we're working - Sam, Sam!' Suzie sighed. 'Bugger it, she's rung off.'

'What's the problem?'

'Nothing.'

'It doesn't look like-'

'Just keep your nose out! It's none of your business.' Suzie sat at the kitchen table with him. 'Sorry,' she said after a few moments.

'That's all right. You sounded upset.'

'I was.'

'Okay.'

'If you must know, it's about you.'

'Me?'

'Yeah, she's got it into her head that we're shagging.' Suzie shook her head. 'As unbelievable as that might sound.' She seemed to realise what she'd said and looked up at him. 'That came out wrong.'

Aidan smiled. 'You don't say.'

Suzie stared at him for a few moments then smiled too. 'She knows I've always dated men before. This is a first for me and...'

Aidan leaned over and squeezed her hand. 'It's okay. I understand. And if you need time...'

She shook her head. 'Don't worry, I'll see her tonight and

smooth it over. The thing is I wouldn't, not to her, not to anyone I'm with, and she knows that. Come on, I need the distraction. After this afternoon…what I saw in the car…' She looked at the laptop. 'What are you searching for? Oh God, not this crap about mules again.'

'It's not crap! You saw!'

'I saw a desperate man who felt there was no way out kill himself. That was it. Full stop.'

'So you're saying all that Finch said was bullshit? Come on, Suzie, remember that old Sherlock Holmes saying?' She looked blank. 'Something about when you've eliminated all the other explanations then whatever's left, however absurd it seems, has to be the truth. Something like that anyway.'

She shook her head. 'I live in the real world. I don't believe in fairy tales.'

'It's scientific-'

'Science fiction then, the result is the same. This was always a wild goose chase. Finch's death has at least closed it off for good. We need to concentrate on the crime and the business front. That's always been the story.'

Shit, Aidan thought. That was the wrong track, he knew it, deep down Suzie probably did too but she was so stubborn. He was getting to know her, there was no point being stubborn back, it just made her even more determined.

He had to find another way.

'Okay,' he said. 'I'll drop this-'

'Good.'

'But only after we do one more thing.'

She sighed. 'Alright, what?'

'We see Jimmy again. Ask him what he knows about the Mule. Let's see what his reaction is.'

'But…'

'Come on, what have we got to lose? An hour tops.'

She nodded. 'All right,' she said. 'One more wild goose to set flapping. By the time we've finished we'll have a fucking flock. Let's go.'

'All right,' he said, and closed the lid of his laptop without shutting it down.

As they left the house, he noticed that someone stood on the street looking at the house. He had a mobile to his ear and turned and walked swiftly away when he saw them.

'Did you see that?' said Aidan.

'Don't worry about it,' said Suzie. 'People are always on the lookout for properties around here. Let's get this over with.'

Aidan got in the car. He hoped she was right. The alternative; that they'd been followed back from the university by Mickey Smith's men didn't bear thinking about.

Chapter Thirty

May 12th 1997 3.16pm

They were in luck. Jimmy was in his 'office', sitting at table in the corner of the bar, three mobiles and a pint on the table in front of him.

'I thought I'd told you two to piss off,' he said.

'We don't give up that easily, Jimmy,' said Suzie.

'Then you're not as smart as I thought you were,' he said. He looked at Aidan's battered face. 'Mickey's blokes do that to you?' he said.

Aidan smiled. 'Nope, it was Mickey himself.'

Jimmy smiled. 'Bleedin' 'ell, you really have got under his skin. And still you've not given up? Well you ain't gonna get anything from me. I told you that last time.'

'Is that because of The Mule?' said Suzie.

The question took Aidan by surprise given her dismissal of Aidan's theory. Jimmy's reaction was even more marked; he froze with his pint halfway to his lips. After a few moments he lowered it down to the table without taking a drink.

'The Mule, Jimmy. Tell us about The Mule.'

Jimmy's eyes darted around the bar. 'For fuck's sake keep your voice down,' he muttered. 'It's not healthy to talk about that.'

'Then keep your voice down when you tell us about him.'

'I don't know nothing.'

'Crap, Jimmy, utter crap. Of course you do.'

'Balls. You can fuck off.'

Suzie smiled. 'We're not going anywhere. We'll sit here and wait until you change your mind.'

'You won't get served. Not unless I say so.'

'So what?' said Aidan. 'The beer's swill anyway. Better off without it.'

'Come on, Jimmy, it'll really cramp your style having us camp out here, following wherever you go,' said Suzie. 'We're not going to give up. It's no skin off your nose, is it? Tell us what you know.'

Jimmy stared at her. 'All right,' he whispered at last. 'But not here, not now. There's too many eyes and ears for my liking.'

Aidan couldn't help but glance around the bar. There were only a handful of customers, mostly elderly, solitary drinkers sipping their way through their pints, apparently paying no attention to anything.

'When and where, Jimmy?' she said.

Jimmy thought for a moment.

'You know the multistorey behind Piccadilly station?'

'Yeah?'

'I'll meet you on the top floor. Nine o'clock.'

Suzie smiled.

'See you there, Jimmy,' she said. 'Come on, Aidan.'

Outside the pub, before either of them could say anything, Suzie's phone rang. She looked at the screen.

'Sam again,' she said. 'Sorry, I need to take this. Hello, love… Yes, yes, I know I said…'

She turned and walked away from Aidan. He gave her privacy.

But, left alone, he had that nasty, all-too familiar feeling of being watched, though by whom, or whether he was right at all, he couldn't say. Odd people were around, singletons, pairs, small groups, there were plenty of cars and vans, many with tinted windscreens parked up in the streets around the pub. It could be any of them - or none.

It was still and unpleasant feeling. He could do without being here. He looked at Suzie. She was still talking on the phone, making the animated hand gestures that many people did to emphasise a point, so odd looking when you thought about it given that the other person couldn't see what was happening, but natural given the emotion.

'Come on, Suzie,' he muttered.

The call continued for another five minutes, during which time the same car, a Vauxhall Astra, drove past them three times, the last time quite slowly, further jangling his nerves.

At last Suzie rang off.

'Sorry,' she muttered. She looked worried, like the cares of the world had dropped on her shoulder.

'You should go to her,' he said.

'But-'

'Just go,' he said. 'Drop me back at the house then go. There's still time.'

Suzie started to say something, then stopped and nodded.

'Yup,' she said. 'Okay. But I'll be back to pick you up later to see Jimmy.'

Aidan nodded. The Astra had parked up about fifty yards away.

'Good,' he said. 'Now can we get out of here?'

'Sure,' she said.

He kept looking over his shoulder all the way back to the car, then did the same when they were driving. He couldn't spot anyone following them but still the disquieting feeling of eyes on them continued to bother him.

Chapter Thirty-One

May 12th 1997 8.16pm

Aidan was beyond worried.

He looked at the clock on the kitchen wall again. It was just after 8.15 pm. Still there was no sign of Suzie.

Without expecting to connect, he called her mobile again. It was as he expected; it was switched off.

He didn't bother leaving a message.

What now? They really should have left for the station by now if they were going to be in time for Jimmy.

Sod it, he couldn't wait any longer. He'd have to fly solo.

He called the local taxi company.

* * *

May 12th 1997 8.56pm

He had the taxi drop him off in front of the station rather than round the back where the multistorey was. It was busy on the concourse despite the hour and mingling with the crowds gave him some cover and made life more difficult for anyone who might be trying to follow him.

The bar to his left was full and noisy. If he wasn't already risking being late he would have called in for a nerve-steadying drink. Ignoring the temptation he followed the car park signs.

He found the stairs and went up until he couldn't go any higher. Breathing heavily from his ascent he checked his watch; two minutes to nine. He'd made it in time.

He opened the door and stepped out into evening. It was still just light but the sky was overcast, threatening rain. It cast a gloomy pall over the parking deck.

There was no-one in sight.

So what now? How long could he loiter up here before security noticed him? There were cameras everywhere. If they were on the ball surely they'd send someone up to have a word with him. He turned to look out at the view, making sure that he was well away from the nearest car. He didn't want them thinking he was a thief looking for a target to break into.

Then he realised that they'd probably put him down as a potential jumper and that this made it even more likely they'd intervene. He walked away from the edge and made his way to the middle of the car park, feeling even more conspicuous.

A jumper. Like Richard.

Richard. God, his death seemed so long ago now but it was still only just over a week. He'd not even had his funeral yet.

Christ, he might not even be able to go.

'So where is she?'

The voice in his ear made him jump.

'Fuck, Jimmy, how long have you been here?'

'Long enough.' Jimmy stepped out of the shadows. 'It was funny watching you. You looked so jumpy I thought you might piss yourself.' He lit a cigarette. 'I asked you where she was.'

'At home. She's got problems.'

'Great. I get sent the monkey and not the organ-grinder. Fuck that.'

He turned and walked away.

'You fuck that, Jimmy,' said Aidan. 'You can talk to me so stop pissing around and tell me about The Mule.'

Jimmy stopped.

'You should keep your fucking mouth shut about him,' he said without turning round.

'You said that this afternoon. Why come up here just to say

the same thing? You know something, you were going to tell us. Why are you chickening out now?'

Now Jimmy did turn. 'Who you calling a fucking chicken?' he said.

'You,' said Aidan who was well beyond caring. 'Just fucking well tell me about him.'

Jimmy bristled for a moment, then turned and walked to the parapet. He leaned his forearms on it and stared out into the gathering gloom.

'You just won't leave it alone, will you? You've got no sodding sense,' he said.

'We can't. We're in too deep.'

Jimmy laughed. 'Yeah, out of your depth. Over your fucking heads in shit.'

'I've had enough of this crap, just tell me what you know about him then we can all sod off home.'

Jimmy turned, his back against the parapet. 'All right, I'll tell you, cos the truth is it ain't going to matter. You're already dead, you just don't know it yet.'

'Yeah, yeah, I've heard it all before.'

Jimmy nodded. For a moment Aidan thought he was looking over his shoulder across the car park to the stairwell, so much so that he himself looked but there was no-one there.

Jimmy started speaking again which got Aidan's attention.

'So is she coming? That Suzie?'

'I don't know. Maybe. Just tell me then we're not pissing around waiting. Right?'

'Right then, well The Mule is everyone's biggest nightmare, at least in the hands of someone like Mickey Smith.'

'We know that. But who is he? Really?'

Jimmy turned to look over the skyline of the Northern Quarter again. 'I don't think anyone knows who he really is. Thing is no bugger that talks to him remembers much about it afterwards. That's if they're still breathing, any roads. There are whispers, though. Some say he's Albanian, others that he's Russian or Ukrainian or summat. There was one girl who knew him though. I'd forgotten about her.'

'Who was she?'

'Just some street girl. He was her boyfriend for a while, that's what she claimed but she was a big time smackhead, quite far gone. I had her on my books for a while but she had to go. Her looks were fucked anyway.'

Nice, thought Aidan.

'What did she say about him?'

'That he was like a kid, a bit simple. Lived for computer games and his pets. He's mad about animals, loves them, talks to them like they're mates. But he's drugged all the time, up to the eye-balls.'

'What, coke? Heroin?'

'Nope. He's sort of tranquilized, because he's impulsive, got no self-control without 'em. He wouldn't hurt a fly but would cut off someone's head without batting an eye. Weird, eh? Anyroads, that's what she said: that he'd always been in trouble all his life, that he needed someone to tell him what to do cos he had no clue what was right himself.' Jimmy gave a little laugh. 'She weren't that reliable though, so take what she said wi' a big pinch of salt. She'd got clean though, in the end.'

'Where is she now?'

Jimmy shrugged. 'They dredged her out of the canal with a needle still in her arm.'

'But…you said she'd got clean.'

'Yup, but I'm guessing that made her more of a threat.'

'Threat? To who?'

'Who do you think? Mickey. He couldn't have anyone interfering with his precious weapon. When she was just a drugged up piece of skirt she wasn't a worry. When she was clean she was.'

'So what…'

'What do you think happened? He got The Mule to get in her head.'

'But he liked her.'

'Makes no odds. He 'as to do what he's told, dun he?' Jimmy turned again and sighed. 'That's what he does. He gets in your head, The Mule. He speaks to you…whispers in your ear and then… I mean, I've no idea how it works but it does. It's enough to make you walk off tall buildings. You know that.'

Aidan nodded. 'Yeah, I've seen it happen. More than once. Today, in fact.'

'Today? Who was the lucky bloke?'

'Mitchell Finch.'

'Who? Oh, was he the shit who was with the Kraut? The ones who brought The Mule to Smith? What happened to him?'

'He drove his car under the back of a truck. Took his head off.'

Jimmy gave another laugh. 'Serves him right, greedy twat. Pair of greedy twats in fact. It was like givin' Hitler the atom bomb when they went to Smith.'

'Do you know what happened to Beck? The…er…Kraut.'

'Dunno but I can guess. Smith will have sorted him. He does that when people get awkward or are no longer any use to him.' Jimmy pointed his middle and index finger to his temple and cocked his thumb back like the hammer of a gun. 'Poof! Problem gone.' Jimmy looked at his watch then over Aidan's shoulder again. 'I guess she's really not coming, is she?'

Without waiting for Aidan to answer he took out a cigarette and a lighter, clicking the latter twice before, finally, lighting up.

It felt like a performance, that it was rehearsed.

A signal.

'What you up to, Jimmy?'

Aidan scanned the roof of the car park.

'Business, mate,' Jimmy murmured. 'Just business.'

The door to the stairwell swung open and a man walked towards them. Even in the gathering gloom, Aidan could see he carried a gun. He turned to run to the other stair door but that, too opened and another, bigger man stepped out.

He was trapped.

'You bastard, Jimmy.'

'Just common sense, mate. I've no intention of havin' my own chat with The Mule.'

'Mickey says thanks for the head's up,' said the gunman.

'No problem.'

'Where's the woman?'

'Dunno,' shrugged Jimmy. 'I waited as long as I could. Thought you might as well do this one.'

'Cheers, Jim.' The gunman nodded towards the stairs where a camera could be seen, white against the concrete. 'They off?' he said.

'Of course,' said Jimmy.

'Come on,' said Aidan. 'Let's talk...'

The gunman laughed. 'Talk? What the fuck would you like to talk about? The weather? Man United's run in Europe? I don't think so. Turn around, kneel down, hands behind your back.' Aidan stared at him. 'Do it!' the man spat. 'Or I'll shoot you in the fucking face. Your mother would like that, wouldn't she?'

Aidan did as he as told. He shut his eyes.

'I'll be off then,' said Jimmy.

'No, Jimmy, you won't,' said the gunman.

'What, But I...?'

'No buts Jimmy. You were supposed to get them both here.'

'It's not my fault that the silly bitch-'

'Change of plan, Jimmy. In fact, plan B.'

There was a phut. Aidan got sprayed by something wet and there was a thump next to him.

Aidan opened his eyes - and wished he hadn't.

Jimmy lay face up next to him. Where his nose should have been was a hole from which blood fountained, driven by the man's still beating heart.

He turned away from this obscene sight, but then felt something being pushed into his pocket,

Then a gun was pushed into his face. Somehow it looked bigger than it had before.

'Message from Mickey. Thanks for the excuse to finish off Jimmy, he's been wanting to give him a pop for a while. He hasn't finished with you and your girlfriend. Actually, he was sort of hoping that only one of you'd turn up. It means he can have more fun.'

Aidan could feel the man's breath on his ear.

'See you again, kiddo,' said the gunman. 'Oh, and one more thing. The cameras up here may be off but the ones downstairs aren't. Good luck. You're going to fucking need it.'

Then he was gone.

A few seconds later a car started and drove off. Carefully, slowly, attracting no attention.

Only now did Aidan run, away from the crumpled mess that used to be Jimmy, to the stairwell door, the one where the muscle had stood.

But as he reached and opened it he realised that there was something heavy in his jacket pocket that was banging against his hip. Without thinking he plunged his hand into it - and brought out a gun.

He could smell the bitter aroma and knew it had been recently fired.

This was the gun that had shot Jimmy.

Chapter Thirty-Two

Aidan stared at the gun in horror, then dropped it and started down the stairs.

His mind was racing, in turmoil, a mess of images dominated by Jimmy's shattered features and fragmentary thoughts. Why had they shot Jimmy?

The stairwell was well lit and he caught sight of his shirt. Oh God, he was covered in blood and flecks of grey brain material. It was disgusting. What could do that? Wouldn't a bullet normally make a neat hole?

He stopped. There was one important point in there, one that really mattered; why give him the gun? Now the reason why the gun in his face looked bigger, it wasn't the same one. Plan B, that's what the killer had said. This was planned.

Why?

Then it came to him; for the same reason they'd disabled the cameras on the top deck; to frame him for murder. His fingerprints would be on the gun. The police would have no video of Jimmy's murder itself but would have of him leaving covered in blood.

This then was Mickey Smith's idea of 'fun'.

He needed to get the gun back. He turned and ran back upstairs. That would remove one bit of evidence. He'd wipe it clean then chuck it in the canal.

It was still where he'd dropped it. He picked it up and headed down the stairs again. There were still the cameras; he'd have to keep his head down and -

A door marked L4 opened and a couple walked through.

They stared at him. He saw their gaze flick from the blood on his shirt and jacket, to the gun then up to his face.

She gasped. He said; 'Jesus Christ. Don't shoot,' then dragged his partner back through the door.

Aidan had no choice now. He ran.

He ran so hard that he fell down the last flight of stairs. Scrambling to his feet he limped through the door onto the street. There were people everywhere, many stopped and stared at him, one screamed and he realised he still held the gun. Quickly he stuffed it in his pocket and ran, turning to the right, away from Piccadilly which teamed with people, into the Northern Quarter where it was darker.

His phone rang. He ignored it.

There was a patch of darkness ahead, to his left. He crossed the street. A mill building, disused, derelict, lay there. There were hoardings around it, a few for sale signs but they'd been there for so many years that, in places, there were gaps like rotten teeth in an old man's mouth. He forced his way through one of the gaps. His feet crunched through discarded syringes, ignored the tug of brambles, the smell of shit and piss and he groped his way to the steps to the mill entrance. At last, with the boarded up door to his back, he sank down, gasping for breath.

But gulping in air was too much. He had to get up, quickly and lean over the railings of the stairs. He threw up, long, hard and painfully expelling everything in his stomach. It almost felt like drowning.

At last he was able to sink back down again.

He hunched forward, his hands resting on the top of his head. He stank of blood and vomit, a winning combination.

He could hear the sirens. The police would be heading to the car park. They'd soon find the body and -

A pulsing blue light illuminated the hoarding. Had someone seen him break in? No, it was just a police car passing by, probably taking a short-cut to the Piccadilly station. At the end of the road it's siren started, presumably because it had come to traffic. The lights and the noise retreated.

His phone rang again, loud in the darkness. Quickly he pressed the reject button to stop the noise.

It was only a few moments later that he thought to look at the display; Suzie.

Maybe this was his lifeline.

He called her back.

'Aidan, what the fuck is-'

'They shot Jimmy,' he said. 'They fucking shot him. I'm covered in his blood.'

'What? Have the police come yet?'

'I'm running. Hiding.'

'But why are you-'

'They set me up. They've planted the gun on me. People have seen me.'

Suzie went quiet.

'Where are you?' she said at last.

'A mill, a derelict one, in the Northern Quarter.'

'Can you get a taxi back to the house?'

'Looking like this? I've got blood and brains in my hair for fuck's sake.'

'Yeah, but I can't leave Sam. I've only just got her settled.'

'I don't give a toss. You need to come and get me. Now.'

There was another pause.

'Alright,' she said. 'Where are you?'

Aidan thought. What was the name of this mill? He must have driven past it a thousand times. Had he ever looked?

'I'm off Old Mill Street somewhere,' he said. 'Lampwick Lane maybe.'

'Okay. I'm on my way. Though I might not have a home to come back to when I'm done.'

Tough shit, he thought.

'I'll call when I'm nearer. See you in about twenty,' she said and rang off.

He put the phone down next to him on the steps so he could both see and hear when it rang.

Ending the conversation deepened his isolation and a wave of tiredness swept over him. He was exhausted; why was he so spent?

It would be the adrenalin working it's way out of his system, he decided. His body had gone into flight mode after the shooting, given him that extra boost to escape the predator. Now he was paying the price.

Now he was alone in the darkness with just the sirens for company. And the rustle of rats nearby.

A few days, that was all it had been, a few days ago his life had been normal. Yes, it was shit, it had been going nowhere but now he craved to have it back again. Then, he was warm and safe in his flat, able to talk to anyone, go to the pub, watch the telly, have a crap undisturbed. Now he couldn't go home, he was an exile living in someone else's house. He had thought that bad but now he was reduced to this; cowering in the filth, cowering in the doorway of a condemned building with a murder weapon in his pocket.

Shit, the gun!

He'd forgotten about it but now he'd remembered he couldn't feel anything else. It was like it was made of lead rather than steel.

He needed to get rid of it.

But where?

The canal would be best but that meant leaving the safety of his hiding place. It was about three streets away. He was still covered in blood. But it was quiet. His chances of being seen wouldn't be high but knowing his luck, he'd blunder out in front of a patrol car or something.

Here then. He could hide it somewhere on the site. Yes, if he wiped it clean then threw it into the bushes, the chances are it would never be found.

But as he took it from his pocket he heard voices, a man and a woman.

'Not here.'

'Where then?'

'In here. Behind the fence.'

To Aidan's horror he heard them start to scramble up into the site, coming through the same gap he had. From the orange glow of the few street lamps that still remained on the neglected back lane he had a clear view of them; him dressed in something dark, her in a short skirt, little leather jacket and boots. A street girl with a punter? God they were close, thirty, forty yards at best. He could hear the zip as she squatted in front of him and pulled down his flies and the sigh of pleasure from the man.

Aidan barely dared breathe.

His phone lit up and the Nokia chimes were as loud as an orchestra in the quiet squalor of the doorway. He scrambled to silence it but knocked it further away.

'What the fuck?'

'It's a fucking peeping Tom!'

'I'll fucking brain him.'

The girl had stood up, the man zipped himself away and was now advancing on Aidan. He managed to grab his phone and stand up , moving away from the steps to try to find a way out.

'You fucking shithead, I'll give you - fuck.'

The man, with the street girl behind him, stopped and his look had changed from anger to fear.

'Don't shoot,' he said. 'I didn't mean anythin' by it, feller, You took me by surprise.'

The girl said nothing but her eyes were wide and her mouth had dropped open.

Aidan looked down. His bloody hand held the gun and it was pointing in the general direction of the pair. He had a flashback to the impact the bullet had on Jimmy's face and shuddered.

'Get over here,' he said. 'On the steps.'

'Okay, okay, whatever you say, boss.'

'Kneel down, facing the building.'

Now the girl did speak.

'No, no, no, no,' she said, over and over.

'Shut up and do as you're told.'

They did.

'Jesus Christ, Jesus Christ,' muttered the man. 'Please, I've got kids.'

They're terrified, thought Aidan. I'm terrifying them. I've got the power to do this.

In this moment I'm Mickey Smith.

It felt…good.

Enough of the crap.

'Stay there,' he said. 'Stay right there and you'll be okay. But move and I'll plug you, yeah?'

'Yeah. We'll stay, boss, won't we, love?'

Aidan didn't wait for her reply. He edged back to the gap in the fence, his eyes fixed on the pair.

His phone, which had stopped ringing, started again. He looked at the display: Suzie.

He answered it.

'Where are you? I'm on Lampwick Lane. I can't see-'

'Coming,' he said and stepped through the gap and down onto the street.

Suzie's car was just a few yards away.

He got into the passenger seat.

'Fucking hell, Aidan. What are you doing waving that around? Are you mad? You should-'

'Just drive,' said Aidan. 'Get me the hell out of here.'

He was shaking as he put the gun back in his pocket.

Chapter Thirty-Three

May 12th 1997 11.06pm

The red water faded as it ran off him and plunged down the plughole.

He wished the memories faded as quickly. The warmth of Jimmy's blood as it had fountained over him, the remains of his face in the half-light, the look on the couple's face on the stairs and the fear of the girl and her punter as he'd brandished the gun at them. They were still all too vivid.

At last the water ran clear, but he stayed under the flow for another five minutes before getting out of the shower and towelling off. When he had clean clothes on, he picked up the bin bag he'd put the ones he'd just taken off in and went downstairs. Suzie was in the lounge.

'I need to find somewhere to put these,' he said. 'Somewhere where they won't be found.'

Suzie nodded at him and handed over a tumbler half full of amber liquid. He smelt it; scotch, one of her uncles single-malts. He took a sip. It was very welcome.

'Can you tell me what happened now?' she said.

He nodded and sat down on the sofa.

'Jimmy got shot,' he said.

'For fuck's sake, I know that. How did it happen? Did they follow you?'

'No. Jimmy shopped us. He told Mickey Smith where we'd be, that's why he chose the car park. He knew it would be quiet at that time of night.'

'The bastard. He deserved what he got.'

The freeze-frame image of Jimmy laying next to him, the blood still fountaining out of the ragged hole came straight back.

'No, no-one deserved that,' he said. 'He was shit scared of Mickey but even more of The Mule.'

Aidan told her about what Jimmy had said in the last few minutes before the hitman arrived.

Suzie pulled a face.

'It's a myth, it has to be. Mickey's just found a way of building up-'

'The Mule's not a myth. For God's sake, Suzie, you've got the evidence of your own eyes, you saw the effect on Finch.'

'Yes, but-'

'And then with Jimmy. We saw him before without any problem. Yeah, he didn't say much but he still saw us. But as soon as we mentioned The Mule he scurried off to Smith pleading innocence and giving us up as proof of his harmlessness.'

Suzie had a whisky of her own in her hand. She took a sip then stared into its depths.

At last she nodded.

'It didn't do him any good. They shot him anyway,' she said.

'They may have let him live if we'd both turned up. That was probably plan A.'

Suzie nodded again, then gave a wry smile. 'For once one of Sam's tantrums did me some good.'

'Yes, by the sound of it, it did.'

Suzie took another sip, then frowned and looked up at Aidan. 'That was plan A, so he moved to plan B? The hitman?'

'Yes, he actually said that. Why?'

'Jesus Christ, this was pre-planned? If we didn't both turn up, this was what they intended?'

'Yes, I think so, to frame me and...' his words trailed off. 'Fuck,' he muttered.

Suzie sprang to her feet.

' Oh my God, because Jimmy told them everything he knew about me. And Sam! Why the fuck didn't you say anything before. Shit!'

'Suzie, I didn't-'

What he didn't remained unsaid as Suzie was already in the hallway. She dashed out the front door without closing it and, by the time he'd reached it, was already showering the house with gravel as she tore out of the drive.

Aidan watched the taillights reach the end of the road and vanish.

Only then did he turn and go back into the house.

Was it safe here? He thought about the man who'd been at the end of the drive before they'd left to go and find Jimmy earlier. Frankly, he was so tired he was beyond caring. He needed to sleep.

And to drink more whisky.

Still, he double-locked the door before he left the hallway. In the morning he had a bag of clothes and a gun to dispose of.

Chapter Thirty-Four

May 13th 1997 8.45am

He woke with the sun in his eyes and a pain like a meat-cleaver through his skull, fully dressed, sprawled across the bed. The first thing he saw was the empty whisky bottle. The second was the bag of clothes and the gun. He groaned; so much for his resolution to bury them in the night.

Well he needed coffee and a shower - in that order - before he could do anything.

As the scalding hot beverage worked its magic gradually he was able to think. They should end this now, pull the plug on investigating just as Richard had four years ago. They had given it their his best shot but come up short. No, it was worse than that, people were dying; Finch, Jimmy. Okay, not innocents but still human beings with a right to life.

And, in Jimmy's case, there was the threat that hung over Aidan himself; the fingerprints on the gun, the eye-witnesses.

Shit, he was in deep shit. He'd made it worse by threatening the couple on the derelict site. Would they have reported it? Maybe not, the guy was being sucked off by a street girl, he'd mentioned kids. Was he married? Would he want to admit what he was doing? Would she?

There was still the other couple; the one in the stairwell. They'd seen him bloody and also holding the gun.

And the CCTV.

And the people in the street.

Shit, he should run.

He almost did.

Instead he took another hit of coffee. His eyes fell on his laptop, still open and plugged in where he'd left it the previous afternoon. That seemed a long time ago now.

He went over to it and pressed the spacebar. It came out of hibernation; his search on 'The Mule' still displayed.

He almost cleared it, closed the page down but something caught his eye, a name; Asimov.

It triggered something in his mind. Asimov, the sci-fi author, he'd read some of his novels in his teens. There was something else, something buried in a corner of his mind that he just couldn't reach.

He clicked on the link where Asimov was named and it all came back.

The Mule was the anti-hero of the early Foundation novels, the mutant who could manipulate people to his will by the force of his mind. Was Beck or Finch a Sci-Fi fan? Possibly, academics tended towards geekiness; he could visualise Finch coming up with the name to dub the product of an Eastern Bloc military research programme.

It fitted too, as far fetched as it sounded, this was a real Mule, someone who could influence people just by talking to them. It was frightening as a concept; in the hands of someone like Mickey Smith it was terrifying.

Surely not? Surely not a real 'Mule'.

But everything he'd seen and heard fitted; the blond man at the accident persuading the police to release Smith; at the hospital with the widow, a few whispers enough for her to change her story; Finch, driving off to decapitate himself after his encounter. What Jimmy had said; Smith had suddenly become invulnerable, able to do anything he wanted. And, in the legitimate world, Urbania able to complete projects that were impossible for others.

Sherlock, albeit another fictional character, said it best:

Once you eliminate the impossible, whatever remains, no

matter how improbable, must be the truth.

Shit, shit, shit. They never had a chance. Richard didn't either.

Suzie was right to worry about her and Sam last night, though, as she still doubted the powers of The Mule, she was probably more afraid of assassins than what a weedy blond Armenian or Ukrainian or Pole could do to her and her lover.

He should warn her.

There was a clatter from the front door that made him jump. He leaned back so he could see into the hallway; it was just a newspaper that had been pushed through the letterbox.

He went back to his musing.

The house phone rang, making him jump. It was the first time it had rung since he'd been there. After his initial shock he left it be. It presumably was for Suzie's Aunt and Uncle, or else a sales call. Whoever it was was persistent for it carried on ringing. When it eventually stopped - presumably it had an automatic cut-off - it started again immediately. The third time it did, Aidan, unable to concentrate with the noise, finally answered the cordless extension in the kitchen.

'Hello?' he said.

'Mr Hughes. Are you enjoying your stay in your home away from home?'

Aidan swallowed. It was Mickey Smith.

'How did you-'

'This is my city, Hughes, I told you that. You weren't that hard to track down.'

Aidan said nothing. He wasn't sure he could speak.

'You seem shocked. I don't know why, you must have known that I'd find you eventually. The net's closing in, Mr Hughes.' Aidan looked out of the patio window, half-expecting to see a squad of heavies or the hitman closing in, so Smith's next words came as a surprise. 'Have you read the paper yet?'

'The paper...?'

'Yes. I had one delivered to you. It makes interesting reading.'

Aidan looked at the paper on the hall floor. After a few moments he went and picked it up.

There, in his own newspaper, was his face, the photo lifted straight from the paper's personnel files. Next to it was a grainy but quite clear frame from one of the security cameras in the car park of him carrying the gun.

The headline read: 'Reporter sought after gangland shooting'.

'You sound like you've read it now, Mr Hughes. Have you shit yourself yet? What did you do with the gun? Throw it in the canal? Bury it in the garden? Whatever, it will be found and traced back to you. The end's coming, Hughes. What does that feel like?'

'But…but…I didn't do it.'

'Yes, that makes it even more delicious. I was just going to have you rubbed out, but then I thought no, that would have been too easy. It's much better this way.'

'Why?'

'You'll suffer longer.'

'But Suzie knows…'

'You think I can't take care of Ms Regan? It's a shame she didn't turn up last night. The idea was to frame you for both her and Jimmy's shooting, but one out of two isn't bad.'

'What have you done with her?'

Smith laughed. 'Me? Nothing, yet. But I will.'

Aidan's legs suddenly buckled and he had to grab at the kitchen counter to stop himself falling. He sank down onto one of the high backed bar stools.

'Ah, it sounds like it's sinking in. That's good.'

'Leave her alone.'

'What can you do to stop me?'

Aidan swallowed. 'I'll tell them, the police, about you, about The Mule. I have the dossier on you–'

'The one Richard Tasker put together and supposedly destroyed?'

'Yes.'

'Let's leave that for a minute, let's go back to Ms Regan.'

'What about her?'

'You fancy her, don't you? You think you've got a chance with her. Why? Because Tasker was shagging her, you think you should do the same? You want to be him, don't you? A good reporter, a man's man? Pathetic.'

'I don't, and Suzie's with Sam.'

'So if she came on to you, you'd say no?'

'No...I...'

'I can make it happen. I have The Mule, remember?'

For a moment Aidan thought Smith was serious but then he laughed.

'No, that will have to remain a wet dream of yours, Hughes,' Smith said. 'But you like her, you wouldn't like to see anything happen to her, would you?'

'Of course not.'

'It will, unless you do as I say.'

'What do you want me to do? Turn myself in? Confess to Jimmy's murder?'

'You'll do that anyway.'

'You can't expect-'

'Yes, I do expect because I'll give you the same promise I gave Mr Tasker four years ago, that if you don't keep quiet I will systematically take away everyone you love. With him it was that same young colleague of his but you've got family, haven't you? Your mother and father live in Preston don't they? Your sister and her young family run a bar in Spain? I'd just need to say the word, Mr Hughes, you know that, don't you? Four years ago I was just going to use my normal people, now I have The Mule. He gives me much more scope for more...ah... imaginative solutions.'

Aidan closed his eyes. The nightmare was reaching its climax.

'Of course, you'll be held in prison on remand whilst they

investigate last night. Can you imagine the reach I have wherever you're sent? Not just amongst the inmates either. They really ought to pay prison officers more. It would make them less open to persuasion, don't you agree?'

'Yes,' said Aidan dully.

'Well, as much as I'm enjoying this little chat - and I really am enjoying it - it's time to end it. Speaking of which, have you thought of that as an alternative to where you're going? No? Well perhaps you should. But first I want the dossier.'

'What?'

'There's not enough in it for you to go public but that's not the point. I don't like loose ends and, if it got out, there'd be questions. I can't have that.'

'But -'

'No buts. The Mule and his minder are parked up outside where Suzie and her bitch live. They're just waiting for the word from me to go in.' Aidan reached for his mobile. 'Don't think of calling them to warn them as I'm sure you were. I'll just kill both them anyway.'

Aidan put his mobile down.

'What do you want?' he said.

'Get the dossier - all of it, I'll do what I promise if I find there's so much as a page missing - and put it outside on the front doorstep. My men will pick it up. You have five minutes.'

Aidan glanced across at the kitchen table where the box file sat. He had a lump in his throat, that was all he had left of Richard, it was his friend's last great work.

'Goodbye, Mr Hughes. And I mean that as a final farewell.'

Smith rang off, leaving Aidan staring at the handset, unable to move.

Eventually he forced himself.

He had no choice, he had to give it up, and quickly. What could he do? Tear pages out? No, he had his camera. He grabbed his compact, it had a half used 24 shot film in it. He quickly flicked through the pages, taking photos as he went, concentrating on the most damning parts, including Richard's scrutiny of the weeks after Mickey took over and the transcript of Hanif Mohammed's interview. All too soon the film ran out and the auto rewind spooled the exposed film back into the canister. The sound was like a requiem for Richard.

He closed the file, then carried it to the front door. With a sigh he placed it on the step and closed the door, stepping back into the hall and slumping down onto the floor, his back to the door.

He didn't have long to wait. Footsteps crunched on the gravel, getting louder as they reached the door, then receding as the dossier was retrieved.

With it Aidan's hopes faded.

And, as he sat there, wondering what Suzie would say, the phone rang again.

He got up and answered it.

'Yes?'

'You really are stupid, aren't you Hughes?'

'What? But I did as you said.'

'I meant about Ms Regan. Do you think I wouldn't have done something about her first? She's far more dangerous than you.'

'You mean - '

'What a surprise; yes, I lied. I sent The Mule to her and her friend last night. Not only did you give up the only evidence you had on me for nothing but you're also now entirely alone.

'This really is goodbye this time, Hughes.'

Smith rang off.

Chapter Thirty-Five

May 13th 1997 9.50am

He was so paralysed with fear that it was an effort to get to his feet. But once he had he wasn't sure what he was going to do; he had to do something, but what?

Hand himself into the police? That was surely the best bet, he'd rely on British Justice. But was that something he could do? They'd not just accept his word, they'd probably arrest and gaol him whilst they investigated. He thought of Mickey Smith's words about the power he held inside and he shuddered.

There was his family too. The threat to them was more than words, it was all too real. He had no doubts it would be followed up on. It was beyond doubt; Aidan would be forced to lie, to confess to a murder he didn't commit.

He found himself upstairs, in the box room. On the floor was the bin bag with the clothes he'd worn last night, the ones he'd intended to bury before he'd hit the bottle. On top was the gun.

He looked at it. Considered. It was an option.

Oblivion.

'No, no, damn you, Smith, I won't, not just to suit you,' he said, and started to pack.

Whilst he did he called Suzie's mobile. He only had Smith's word for it that something had happened to her. He willed her to answer.

Her mobile rang until it went to voicemail.

He completed his packing. The last things that went into the bag were the bin bag and the gun. He wondered if the safety was on, then even if it had a safety catch at all; he had no idea about guns, only that this was a familiar trope of movies. Whatever, even if he couldn't fire it, it might be a useful threat.

A threat. Him threatening people with a gun. What had he come to?

Whatever, he was here and there was no going back.

Where was he going to go?

A bed and breakfast might be okay as long as he paid cash. Luckily he had a fair bit on him.

He looked in the mirror. He'd be recognised like this. What if he cut and dyed his hair? That might help, he'd seen some hair dye in the bathroom, presumably belonging to Suzie's aunt. It was dark brown, different enough from his own light brown, almost fair hair. He'd seen some hair clippers there too. He could dye it then cut it, that would help.

Would he have time? How long before the police found him here?

He didn't know but it was worth the gamble.

He headed for the bathroom.

* * *

May 13th 1997 12.40pm

Nearly two hours later he looked in the bathroom mirror inspecting his handiwork. Not bad; although his cut was a bit rough and ready. After some effort he'd managed to get it fairly even, though doing the back was really hard. His first attempt at hair dying had been messy but largely successful, though stained towels littered the bathroom.

He'd have to buy some new ones for Suzie's aunt if he ever got out of this.

The important thing was that he hardly recognised himself.

Now, where should he go?

He needed to get away from here; Mickey Smith knew where he was. He might still have people watching, though. He'd have to find some way to slip out unobserved.

If only Suzie was still around. She could have picked him up.

With no expectation, he tried her mobile again.

It was a shock when it was answered.

'Hello?'

The voice was uncertain but sufficiently familiar to give him hope.

'Suzie?'

A pause.

'No. It's Susan's mother. Susan is…'

She sounded deeply upset.

'Is she alright?'

There was a rustle at the other end of the line, a muttered conversation. Then a man came on.

'Hello, I'm Suzie's father. Who is this?'

'It's Ai…Alan,' lied Aidan. 'A friend. What's happened?'

'There's been an…incident. An argument I think. Suzie's… er…friend attacked her, then killed herself. With a knife.'

'Oh my God. Is Suzie-'

'We're at the hospital. She's in theatre. It's quite bad. Now, if you don't mind…'

'Of course. If…when Suzie wakes. Tell her-'

But Suzie's father had already rung off.

He puffed out his cheeks. Poor Suzie. And Sam.

That bastard Mickey. Just because he could.

Aidan was going to get him, though he had no idea how.

But this was it. He was alone. He had no one else to fall back on, Richard was gone, Suzie too. If he was going to get Smith it would be a solo effort.

Was he up to it? Well he'd find out.

He had nothing else to lose.

Chapter Thirty-Six

May 13th 1997 2pm

Aidan got a break; there was no sign of anyone watching the house. He could leave without an elaborate plan.

But then he realised what that meant; Mickey Smith had delivered another insult, he didn't consider Aidan a threat anymore. He was dismissed, forgotten already, that was what the message said.

It wasn't a relief, it made him angrier.

* * *

May 13th 1997 6pm

By evening he was in a bed and breakfast in Sheffield. He'd caught a train over that afternoon, paying on the train by cash and keeping a baseball cap that he'd found at the house on all the way. His disguise seemed to hold, no one seemed to pay him much attention, if any. He had paid a little extra for a room with a TV and watched the local news after he'd booked into the B&B; there was nothing about him. That was good, it suggested that the murder was still a Manchester story and hadn't yet spread.

Maybe it wouldn't.

He then switched to Ceefax. After a little scrolling through the pages he found a news article:

'POLICE SEEK REPORTER
AFTER GANGLAND MURDER'

It was all there, the bare details, the murder, the threatening behaviour afterwards in the car park, his name. But nothing about the couple at the mill, it looked like that hadn't been reported.

Thank God that Ceefax was just a text service, he thought. If his photograph had been up there it would have made his life impossible.

A few articles later there was another one.

'WOMAN CRITICAL AFTER KNIFE ATTACK'

Woman, named locally as Susan Regan, 28 is critically ill in hospital after knife attack at home in which another woman, Samantha Graves, died. Police say they are not seeking anyone else in connection with the incident.

Aidan grimaced; 'Police not seeking anyone else', code for a domestic incident, an attempted murder/suicide in other words. Poor Suzie, they didn't even drop the hint that she was the victim, some reading it might assume her to be the attacker. But then it was unfair on Sam too; she'd been used by Smith as a weapon and then had been discarded like throwing a gun in the canal.

The gun. He took it out of his bag and looked at it. It was small, on the barrel was inscribed 'Pietro Beretta' and 'Made in Italy'. It was almost toy-like and if he hadn't seen the effect it had had on Jimmy's head he'd have dismissed it as harmless. There were marks on the barrel where something had been forced onto it, presumably a silencer given the muffled shot that had killed Jimmy. The killer had taken it, wanting it to use again.

He sat on the bed and held it in his hand, his finger on the trigger, arms outstretched, visualising Mickey Smith in the sights.

But could he actually do it?

Really? On another human being, even a bastard like Smith? Aidan shook his head and lowered the gun.

Maybe it would be different for real? No, he knew the truth and he'd stopped lying to himself. He had to find another way.

But what? He had no idea.

His eyes fell on his old work mobile. He'd switched it off after he'd made his escape to Suzie and her aunt and uncle's house, there seemed little point in having it on. He wondered if it had any charge left on it and, for no other reason than that, he turned it on.

It came to life. The battery was on the low side but it had held up reasonably well.

There were a few text messages plus an indication he had voice messages; Mickey Smith's men seemed to have stopped tapping into them, too. He dialled into the message service and started to listen.

The first couple were from Gill, wanting to know when he was coming back to work. That was to be expected. The next was timed at 12.41pm the previous day, he expected that to be Gill too but then he presumed it was an accidental call because the first part consisted of wind noise and heavy breathing. But then someone spoke, gasping the words.

It took a few moments for Aidan to recognise it as belonging to Mitchell Finch.

He thought about the time; 12.41. That would have been about the time Finch bolted, when he was being chased across the car park by Smith's heavies and The Mule. Aidan remembered seeing Finch make a call but presumed it was to the police but now he recognised what had happened; Finch knew the power of The Mule, he'd made one last call whilst he still could and had chosen the reporters, using one of the cards that they had just given him. By chance he'd chosen Aidan's.

It was hard to make out the message that Finch gasped out. He had to listen five or six times before he made out enough to write it down:

'Dot Salford dot uk forward slash intranet forward slash mitchell finch…password one one four seven eight nine em eff.'

That was all Finch said.

At first he'd thought it had to be some code. Sleep deprived as he was it took him sometime before the penny dropped; this was the pass to Finch's files on the Salford staff intranet. The paper had one, it made a lot of sense that universities did too. They held a whole range of files, allowing easy access to the material.

So what was on Finch's? Something important enough for him to spend his last few breaths calling the reporters to give it to them. Was this the key to the whole thing?

But how could he access it? The paper's intranet could, in theory, be accessed remotely but Aidan had never done it. It was easier to do it in person within the building or, in the case of a university, the campus.

Yet he was a wanted man. His photo was in the paper, a paper that was read all over Greater Manchester. That would really push his disguise.

Whilst he was still pondering this, he listened to the rest of his voice messages. There were three; the first from Gill, serious, business-like, but still caring in tone, asking him to come in and explain what had happened, that the paper would stand behind him as much as they could but he needed to come and tell his story.

He gave a mirthless laugh. 'You mean come in and give the paper its exclusive, Gill,' he muttered. 'Sorry, thanks but no thanks.'

The second was much harder to listen to. It was from his parents, his mother first, in tears, telling him the police had been to see them, then his father taking over; 'Son, please, for your mother, for me, give yourself up. Whatever problems you're in, it can be sorted out…'

He stopped listening; it was too much to bear.

He almost didn't listen to the last one expecting it to be more of the same, or a message from the police.

It wasn't either; it was from Roisin.

'Aidan, I don't care what they say, I know you didn't kill anyone. You have your faults but I know you and I know you couldn't do this. If you need a friend, if you need somewhere to stay then you can come to me. No strings, no conditions. I wouldn't turn you in. Call me if you need me.'

Now he was overwhelmed. He couldn't help himself as it all caught up with him. He lay back on the bed and sobbed.

Chapter Thirty-Seven

May 14th 1997 7.50am

Aidan caught the 7.07am train from Sheffield to Manchester. There were earlier ones but he thought it would be easier to hide amongst the commuters rather than be virtually alone in the carriage. This was the express, the only stop before Piccadilly was in Stockport and this was where he got off.

Roisin was waiting in her car outside as arranged. Baseball cap pulled down to hide his face, Aidan was in and they were away in moments.

'You holding things together?' she said.

'Just about.'

'You promise you'll tell me everything?'

'Yes. When we get in.'

'Okay. Sleep if you need to. You look shattered.'

Aidan nodded and closed his eyes.

He wasn't going to sleep though.

* * *

May 14th 1997 11.05am

Roisin puffed out her cheeks and shook her head.

'That's quite a story, Aidan,' she said. 'It's hard to believe. Almost as hard to believe as your hair colour.' She grinned at him, trying to lighten the mood he assumed.

His mood stayed grim.

'It's the truth.'

She nodded slowly. 'I know, and I didn't say I didn't believe you, particularly with what this suggests,' she patted the fourteen photos of Richard's dossier on the kitchen table, not all of them were clear, Aidan had had them developed at a one-hour photo place, these were all that he'd had left on the roll. 'But there's not a lot, is there? The police will struggle to take it seriously. Even if you had the whole thing, you have to admit it does sound far-fetched. Mind control? Really?'

'I know. It sounds crazy. But I've seen The Mule work. He's real. It's real.'

Roisin didn't reply immediately. She just stared at the file as if trying to make it give up its secrets by the sheer force of her mind.

'Are you having second thoughts,' he said at last. 'You could be in big trouble by taking me in.'

Now she looked at him. 'Aidan, I've had second, third, fourth and fifth thoughts since you called me,' she said. 'Yet you're still here, aren't you? Let's just assume I've gone soft in the head. If I get arrested, I'll plead insanity.' She looked at the file again. 'We're both committed now. We need to get you off. You need more evidence.'

He nodded.

'Maybe it will be in Finch's files. On the intranet.'

Roisin nodded.

'I did my degree at Salford,' she said. 'I know my way around.'

'I can't ask you to-'

'No you can't but you can't go out, can you? I'm doing it anyway.'

'Thanks, I-'

'It's not just for you, Aidan, it's for me.' She looked into his eyes. 'I'm going out on a limb based on the fact that I've decided I trust you. I need more proof that my judgement is right or just confirmation that I've really gone Tonto like my sensible side is screaming at me.' She smiled. 'Sorry.'

He smiled back.

'No need to apologise,' he said.

She looked at her watch.

'Right, no time like the present. Write down Finch's login details and I'll drive over there.'

He did as he was asked.

Chapter Thirty-Eight

May 14th 1997 2.40pm

Waiting was bad for his nerves. Every noise outside Roisin's flat made him jump; the slamming of a door, footsteps on the stairs, even the flushing of a toilet, all were reminders that there were people nearby. Even if they weren't Smith's men creeping around, as a wanted man everyone was a potential threat to him.

Then there was the street. Roisin lived right in the heart of the city, in one of the new residential developments that had sprung up which were repopulating what had been a wasteland. That meant busy streets, lots of traffic, places for watchers to hide. Every five minutes he cautiously pulled the blinds aside to check whether anyone was lingering longer than they should, or that a suspicious black BMW was parked up with a view of the flats.

There were some false alarms but nothing concrete.

It was hard though. The realities of his situation were sinking in. Wanted by the police, face splashed across his own paper accused of being a murderer - an accusation made almost as good as conviction by the publicity - and with Mickey Smith, The Mule and more conventional hitmen waiting in the wings to finish him off if, by some miracle, he escaped the charge.

It was pretty hopeless. Yet he still stood whilst those around him, the people he'd worked with or talked with, Richard, Suzie, Jimmy, Finch, were either dead or as good as. Could he carry on to save his own skin? Should he? Was he just going to add Roisin, his parents, his sister to the list of casualties?

He was still on this train of thought when he heard the key

in the door.

It was Roisin.

She held up several computer disks.

'I've got it,' she said.

* * *

May 14th 1997 3.43pm

An hour or so later, they sat in front of Aidan's laptop. They'd read pages and pages of research papers and notes. All were interesting but one file had the most impact, perhaps because of its media. It was an audio file that took up most of one of the floppies, indeed it was the main reason why Roisin had had to go to the university's shop to purchase more.

'Let's listen again,' she said.

He pressed play and Finch's voice came out of the laptops pathetic, tinny sounding speaker.

What Finch said came over like a lecture, which was no surprise, but it was, at least, more riveting than any Aidan could recall from his own student days.

'It started with something I believe we have all observed,' said Finch. 'That some people are better at persuading people to do things than others. These people are life's natural sales people, able to clinch deals where no-one else can, or politicians able to take the population on a journey even if the dream they are selling is abhorrent.

'Yes, I am thinking of Hitler. People who witnessed him said he was an almost hypnotic speaker, it was not just what he said but the way that he said it, the rhythm, the cadence, the rise and fall of his voice, it was almost mesmerising. Don't forget, unlike the other dictators of the era, Lenin, Stalin, Franco or Mao, Hitler was voted into office, he persuaded millions by personal appearances and via the radio thanks to Goebbels.

'He was not the only one though. There have been others, not just in politics but in all walks of life and there will be more again, those with an unusual ability to convince others to do things, things that, otherwise they would not do, even abhorrent, evil acts. It occurred to some that this ability to persuade could be something that was inherent in some people. If it was then this could become an evolutionary advantage. It could also be used as a weapon.

'The research into this started in Germany the late 1930s and continued into the war years. I think you can guess where the bulk of it took place. The East German government that took over in 1945 decided that this was something worth continuing the research.

'The programme was on the fringe of science, indeed some within the DDR considered it as little more than superstition and witchcraft. Whatever, they recruited doctors to carry out tests and surgical procedures on subjects they identified as showing promise to see if the powers of persuasion could be enhanced. Some of these procedures were barbaric, as might be expected in the Nazi death camps. These procedures continued as the doctors who previously worked in the camps were rounded up and put to work after the war. There were many deaths, more subjects were reduced to a vegetative condition, but still the research went on. It did because there were successes, primarily from one family line that showed promise.

'From the records I have seen, this bloodline was treated like it was some kind of pedigree animal, a dog or a cow. There was a programme of interbreeding enhanced by surgery. This had the hoped-for results in terms of the subjects ability but caused the usual problems of interbreeding; congenital illness, death and mental disorders.

'The man known today as The Mule is one and possibly the only survivor of the programme. Even then he nearly slipped the net. When the research was officially stopped after the fall of communism, he was placed in an institution, for this man, known only as Josef B, was diagnosed as being autistic by those who discovered him in the lab. He was only happy when working with animals which the DDR researchers had allowed him to do but this was taken away from him when he was institutionalised.

'It was a big mistake. Josef broke out. Actually 'broke out' is not accurate; the night staff just let him go, though, afterwards, they had no idea why they had done so. They were fired.

'Josef was found a few days later on a farm. He'd persuaded the farmer to give him board and lodgings and was happily working with the cows and sheep. The farmer's wife saw Josef's picture on the news and informed the police. When they came to arrest him, one dropped dead on the spot after talking to him whilst another shot himself. In the end they had to tranquillize Josef with a dart gun like he was a dangerous wild animal.

'This time the authorities had no choice. They had to call in members of the DDR research team. The one they found with the cleanest hands was Gerhard - Dr Beck.

'He undertook to assess Josef. He was given accommodation for both of them at the hospital. After working there for six months and with an apparent improvement in Josef's behaviour, they were allowed to leave with Josef under Beck's guardianship.

'What the authorities in the West did not know was how Gerhard controlled The Mule. The truth was shocking, it took a while for Dr Beck to admit it to me and, even then, I found it difficult to accept.'

'You still bloody well did though, didn't you,' muttered Roisin. 'Amazing how people's morals change when there's lots of money involved.'

Aidan just nodded and continued to listen to what the late Dr Finch was saying.

'...surgically implanting electrodes deep in The Mule's brain. This could be operated remotely and, at the flick of a switch, The Mule could be made to experience deep, physical pain, the level of which could be determined by the operator. The DDR research team had worked on conditioning Josef as if he was a lab rat. Eventually they developed him to the point where he was completely cowed and where the mere sight of the control box was enough to persuade Josef to do exactly what he was told. He still had some free will and needed sedation to stop him running but he was conditioned not to harm himself - some of the earlier subjects had escaped by suicide - and to obey the box holder.

'This was what the original institution did not know, but Josef was clever enough to know that they didn't have the box so he was free to escape. When Dr Beck arrived the first thing he did was show Josef it. The mere sight was enough to turn Josef back into The Mule, a docile, but deadly weapon - in the wrong hands.

'It was at this point that Gerhard came to Britain. What choice did he have? The German universities would not employ him, he had no income save the pittance the state gave him to look after Josef. It was stupid of them, so short sighted that they could not see what they had. He brought Josef with him, found him a job on a farm. The Mule proved not to be at all stupid, he quickly learned English.

'I saw it straightaway when I got to know Gerhard and heard about The Mule. I could see what he could do.'

'You pompous arsehole,' said Roisin. 'You deserved what you got.'

'Probably,' said Aidan. He paused the recording and skipped on, mainly because he remembered that the next five minutes were mainly Finch complaining about his treatment by the university, his being overlooked for promotion, and then the reaction after they'd set up Astcanza and the University's due diligence process threw up questions about Beck's past. He judged whether he'd gone far enough, then hit 'play' again.

'...so had no choice but tell them to stuff their tenure and resigned. It was intolerable-'

'Just shut up, you wanker,' muttered Rosin.

'He's about to get to the bit about going to Smith,' said Aidan.

'The obvious thing to do was to go to the private sector for funding,' said Finch. 'I had worked with Mr Smith before on his casino project. He had run into frustrating blockages with the authorities. I knew, with coaching and proper instruction, The Mule could help him. I assumed that Smith was a legitimate businessmen. I had no idea then about his er, other, activities. If I had, of course I wouldn't have gone to him. I hope people understand that and sympathise with my position.'

By the look on Roisin's face, it was clear that people did not understand and there was little or no sympathy. Aidan had to agree with her; Finch would have had to have been wilfully blind not to see the truth about Mickey Smith. That nickname of his; Eichmann, really was fitting.

'Mr Smith was, of course, sceptical but he let us stage a demonstration on a development project his building company had their eyes on. When we obtained a sale at very advantageous terms from the developer who owned it he was impressed. By the time the negotiations with the council, the tenants and the interest groups were complete, he was excited.'

'That was Maxwell Mill,' said Aidan.

Roisin nodded.

'It all looked good at first. Gerhard and The Mule were provided with accommodation, we all received a generous allowance. We assumed Smith would be our first client, the first of many. It was only later that we realised what his intentions were. It was complete control.'

There was a pause in the recording. The first time Aidan had thought it had ended but then heard Finch's breathing in the background. When he started talking again there was a break in his voice.

'I did not realise how ruthless a man Smith was. Dr Beck… vanished…after a few months. I was told not to enquire any more. Then I was squeezed out, forced to give up control of my own company by…'

Finch's voice trailed off. Aidan guessed that the academic could not bear to say the words explaining just what Smith held over him.

'I was just grateful to escape with my life. Though it has been an exquisite form of torture waiting, just waiting for him to tire of me.

'This is where I had the idea of this set of documents, this testament which can be my legacy. The legacy of a decent man so cruelly betrayed by-'

'Oh for fuck's sake, enough,' said Roisin and closed the laptop down to silence Finch.

Aidan couldn't blame her.

Chapter Thirty-Nine

May 14th 1997 9.35pm

Later that evening, after Aidan had written up his notes and they'd eaten, they sat in Roisin's lounge. He knew she wanted to say something. He wondered what it was.

'So,' she said. 'What now?'

Aidan looked at the disks, and his laptop with the audio files, now fully documented, then onto the photos, all that remained of Richard's dossier.

'What do you mean?' he said. 'We take this to the police.'

Roisin shook his head. 'Aidan,' she said. 'I'm sorry. It's still not enough.'

'But what Finch said, Beck's files-'

'Finch is dead. Beck is dead. Richard too. Suzie's not dead yet but who knows whether Smith will let her live for long. You said yourself the police deal in facts, not stories.' she sighed. 'You need to do the same, Aidan. Accept the facts.'

He took a deep breath. He looked at the evidence again. She was right, he knew she was. Still he clutched at the last straw.

'I was hoping for a lot more, something that would definitely tie Smith to a crime, documentary proof. That isn't there, it's just Finch's opinion. But there's The Mule himself. Isn't he being held against his will? That's a crime, isn't it?'

Roisin nodded, her face grim. 'Yes, it is but he's controlled, Finch said so. If they ask him he's not going to tell them the truth, is he?'

The last straw slipped away as if it were covered in oil.

'No,' he said.

'So we're back with the bald facts. They've got a dead body, Jimmy. They've got CCTV of you holding the murder weapon. That's all they need, it's easily enough to put you in prison, whatever you have here. They may find all this interesting but that's probably about it.'

'But...'

'But what? You know I'm right, don't you?'

'Yes,' he said at last. 'You're right. It sounds too far-fetched. But...you really expect me to just give up? After all that's happened?'

'No, you'll go to prison.'

'Yes.'

'That means you'll be under Smith's control,' she said. 'Only surviving at his pleasure. Does that sound inviting?'

'It doesn't but at least I'd be alive. I think that's what he wants, to know I'm suffering. Anyway, if you're right, what's the alternative?'

Roisin sighed and shook her head.

'You know what will happen eventually,' she said.

'But at least everyone else, my mum and dad, my sister, you - will be still alive too. If I can't say anything then there's no reason for him to do anything to them.'

'I never had you down as being so noble.'

Aidan laughed.

'Me neither,' he said.

Roisin didn't laugh. She was frowning. 'There may be another way. It's wrong but...' She looked up at Aidan. 'Look, I'm from a big family in the South, some of them were big in the republican movement. Very big, in fact. They are used to operating outside the law. They could get you a new identity. They've done it before. You might have to stay in Eire for a while but, after that, you could go anywhere.'

'Anywhere except home,' Aidan murmured.

'Yes. That's right. Your life here would be over. You'd never see your family again. I'm sorry. But it would be a new start.'

A new start. It was tempting. But his mum and dad, his sister would still be at risk.

Roisin had probably read his mind.

'Look, don't decide yet,' she said. 'Sleep on it, you look all in. Whatever you do is going to change your life forever. You need a clear head.'

Aidan nodded. He looked at the sofa. 'I am shattered,' he said. 'I can't remember when I last slept properly.'

Now Roisin smiled. 'You don't have to crash there if you don't want to,' she said.

It took a second or so for what she'd said to sink in. Then he took her hand and followed her through to her bedroom.

Chapter Forty

May 15th 1997 7.50am

Aiden had a troubled night, full of wild thoughts, his mind never still. He must have slept eventually for he woke to the alarm with his arm over Roisin. She turned and smiled at him.

'Morning,' she said. 'How are you doing?'

'Not too bad.'

'Liar.' She sighed. 'Have you decided what you're going to do yet? The police or a new identity?'

Aidan shook his head.

'I'm not surprised. Neither are that inviting.' She looked at the bedside clock. 'I should call in sick today.'

'No, go in as normal. We don't want people putting two and two together.'

She frowned.

'I don't like leaving you.'

'I'm alright, promise.'

She looked doubtful. 'You promise? You wouldn't do anything stupid?'

'Suicide, you mean? No, I wouldn't do that.'

'Good, cos I'd kill you if you did.'

He returned her smile, and kissed her as she got up to get in the shower.

He listened to the water running, smelt the moist, warm aroma of her shampoo drifting in from the bathroom and reflected.

He hadn't lied, not really.

Suicide wasn't on his mind.

But his intentions were probably stupid. He had decided though; he didn't really have a choice. Running away wasn't enough, it would still leave everyone he cared for at risk.

There was only one way to end this.

* * *

May 14th 1997 10.52am

His head was pounding, his stomach churned, the after-effects of three nights of little sleep catching up with him. Still though, his thoughts were clear.

Aidan wished his plan had been. It was vague, a long shot, it relied on lots of things coming together but it was still viable, knowing the behaviour of the set.

So he was content to sit and watch from Roisin's car. He was glad she could walk to work; it saved the risk of a hire car. Whatever, Aidan had a good view of the gates and high wall surrounding the house, invisible from the road, shielded as it was by the wall and a stand of trees. There were security cameras, two by the gate, another a little way around the road. Naturally Smith would be careful, always on the watch for intruders with evil intent, hence his vigil.

His mobile rang. It was his 'clean' one. It could only be one person, now.

'Hi Roisin,' he said.

'Hey, how are you doing?'

Just as she spoke, the automatic gate started to open.

'I'm fine,' he said.

'What are you up to?'

'Writing up a few notes, just trying to keep busy.'

His eyes fixed on the gate. A Range-rover with heavily tinted windows came through towing a horsebox.

'That's good.'

'Yes, look, I'm sorry Roisin, I need the loo. Talk later?'

'Yes of cour-'

He'd already rung off because the four-wheel drive had already turned left out of the drive and was heading off down the road.

Aidan started the engine and, from a safe distance, followed it.

* * *

May 14th 1997 2.05pm

Three hours later, he felt the vehicle slow then swing around to the right. This had to be the drive.

The heat inside was intense, made worse by the warmth of the horse's body and the blanket and straw that he was covered by. The animal had stamped his feet nervously all the way back from the woods at Alderley Edge; he guessed that it could sense his presence.

He'd waited until the horse and rider were well clear before he walked over to the car and horsebox. He was relieved to find the latter open, even more so that there was a place to hide within it. It meant that he could use plan A. Plan B was to use threats. He'd always hoped this way of getting inside came off. It was a relief when it did.

The driveway - if that's what it was - was smooth, the trailer hardly bumping at all. Nothing but the best for Smith and his family, of course.

The car stopped, the engine switched off. He heard the door open then slam shut.

'Josef!' A woman's voice. 'Ah, there you are. See to Huntsman. Give him water and then hose him down. He's hot.'

'Yes, madam.'

That voice.

Quiet, subservient, accented, foreign.

Polish?

He heard the horsebox ramp clatter down and the door open, a welcome influx of cooler air swept in. It was welcome, even under the blanket and straw that covered him. The drowsiness that almost dragged him into sleep faded away; he was revitalised in both strength and purpose.

The box swayed as someone stepped inside and uttered soft, calming words. They led the horse out, the trailer tipping slightly under the weight of the heavy animal as it walked down the ramp. Metal shoes rang against stone, receding as they led the horse away.

Now was the time. Aidan threw off the blanket and got to his feet, then cautiously crept down the length of the horsebox and looked out.

As he expected, they were in a yard with stables on either sides. The huge house was a little further away, a sprawling modern mansion, built in a style made popular I the 1930s.

What Aidan hadn't expected was that the first person he saw would be the one he feared most. Not Mickey Smith, but The Mule. He had his back to Aidan, closing the stable door, still talking to the horse.

This wasn't the plan. He hadn't come for The Mule. Now he had no choice. He had to do this.

He walked down the ramp and swiftly across the yard to the stable. He was around ten feet away when The Mule turned and saw him.

He froze, staring at what was in Aidan's hand. The gun that had killed Jimmy.

Chapter Forty-One

May 14th 1997 2.16pm

The safety was off. Aidan knew this because he'd spent time finding his way around the gun, working out what each part was, checking that it was loaded, examining the tiny but evil looking cartridges; soft, grey lead held in brass, a cross cut into each tip presumably to make the projectile open like a flower on impact with flesh and bone.

He thought of this now as his finger was on the trigger, thought of Jimmy with his head torn open, thought of the man who stood in front of him now, the one who was not the intended target of this mad, desperate assassination. The man who was as much victim as weapon, abused all his life and knew he could not pull it.

But he had to do something before the man spoke and used his own deadly weapon; his voice.

'Josef, I haven't come here for you,' he found himself saying. 'I'm not going to hurt you.'

The Mule continued to stare at the gun, his eyes flicking up to Aidan's face. His mouth, weak, the lips pale, began to move.

'Josef, look I'm putting the gun down,' Aidan said quickly, lowering his arm. 'See, I told you, I'm not here for you.'

The Mule was still wary but he'd not spoken. So far at least. Aidan had to try to keep it that way. But how? He hadn't rehearsed it at all.

Close to and in daylight, the man was indeed nondescript; pale, washed out, blond hair thinning, eyes dull. The look in those eyes reminded Aidan of animals in a zoo he'd once made the mistake of visiting during a holiday in Asia, particular in the great apes, a lost, trapped, hopelessness which was distressing and had made him cut short his visit. But this was what The Mule was, what he had been all his life; a lab rat, experimented on, imprisoned for what he was, not for what he'd done. Now he was little more than a slave.

'Other people hurt you, don't they, Josef?' he said. 'They have all your life, haven't they?'

The Mule nodded. It was a small gesture but it was huge, he was getting through.

'It's the same now, isn't it? They hurt you here?'

The reaction this time was different; it was fear. The Mule glanced towards the house, alarmed. Shit, he'd gone too far.

'It's all right, Josef, we don't need to mention that again. I won't say anything more about it.' The Mule turned back to Aidan and opened his mouth. He needed to say something, quickly, to stop The Mule talking, stop him taking Aidan's free will away. 'You like animals, don't you, Josef?' he said. 'You love being around them?'

'Yes,' said The Mule. He turned his head to look at the horse behind him and reach out to stroke it's head. 'Animals don't hurt Josef.'

As a result, he'd gotten him to speak without using the words as weapons. That he had to keep up.

'No, they don't. I like animals as well.'

Did he? He supposed so. Shit, this was like reasoning with a lion and trying to persuade it not to eat you.

'Yes, I know. You are man with dog,' said The Mule.

Dog? What dog? Aidan didn't have a dog.

Then he remembered. The dog that been run over.

'Yes, that's me. I tried to help it.'

'You covered dog with coat. Dog died. Dog should not have died. That wrong.'

A way in. Thank you, God.

'That dog shouldn't have been hurt, should it? Yet, it was. That was Mickey Smith's fault wasn't it?'

The Mule looked blank. How could that be?

'Mr Smith, the man who lives here?' Aidan nodded towards the house.

Now The Mule got it.

'The man with the box,' he muttered. 'Yes. Bad man.'

Aidan was nonplussed. The box? What box?

Wait, what Finch had said about how The Mule was controlled. The electrodes in the pain centres linked to a control box.

'The man with the box, yes. The man who makes you do bad things.'

'Bad things?'

'Hurting people, making them do things they don't want to?'

The Mule just shrugged.

He doesn't care, thought Aidan. Not about people. Yet he called Smith a "bad man". Because he hurt him? No, it was something else. Something The Mule cared about.

'The bad man hurts animals doesn't he?'

The Mule nodded, his face hardened.

'What does he do, Josef?'

'He shoots foxes. He shoots birds. He hits dog with stick. He is very bad man.'

Unbelievable thought Aidan. He can make men jump off buildings, drive under lorries and decapitate themselves and make lovers attack one another without a murmur of disquiet yet, where animals are concerned, it's a totally different matter.

Yet wouldn't Aidan be the same if his life had been like The Mule's? What was he, thirty-five, forty? Forty years of living like a lab rat, no free will, being abused by people. No wonder he preferred the company of animals.

And Aidan must stop referring to him as 'The Mule' even in his head. This was a man. A victim.

'Josef,' he said.

Josef looked up at him.

'Josef, I can help you. You can leave here, I'll get you out.'

'Leave?' He seemed to be struggling with the concept.

'Yes, leave and go and work with animals. On a farm maybe, like you did before.'

'Farm not good. Farmer kills animals.'

'All right then, an animal centre, a home where animals get better.'

Josef smiled. He nodded at the thought.

'Yes,' said Aidan. 'That can happen. Come on, leave the bad man who hurts them.'

Now Josef frowned.

'But man has box. Box hurts Josef. Josef cannot leave.'

'We'll get you away, far away, away from the box.'

'No, no, no, they find me!'

Josef was panicking.

'No, Josef, they won't. We'll go to the authorities, tell them, they'll help you.'

'No, no, no!'

'Josef don't you want this hell to be over?'

The Mule nodded.

'Yes,' he said. 'Over. I want it over.' He looked up at Aidan, then down at the gun. 'You must kill Josef.'

'What?' Aidan stared in disbelief. 'No. I can't do that.'

'Yes, yes. Josef wants.'

'But…No, no I can't.'

'Please.'

'Josef, no. Don't you want to spend your life working with animals instead? Think about it, a rescue centre somewhere, you'd help sick creatures. Doesn't that sound good?'

This seemed to get through. He nodded. 'But man with box-'

'We'll get the box. We'll get the bad man and take-'

Something cold was pushed against the side of Aidan's head. He didn't need to look to know it was the barrel of a shotgun.

'No, I don't think you will, Mr Hughes,' said Mickey Smith. 'I don't think so at all.'

Chapter Forty-Two

May 14th 1997 2.27pm

'I should blow your fucking head off,' said Smith, pushing the shotgun barrels harder against the side of Aidan's neck. 'Coming to my house, *my house*. Who do you think you are?'

'You sent your guys into mine,' said Aidan.

He got a harder push with the barrels that made him stagger.

'Shut it, shithead. I can do that because I'm me, because I can and because you're a worm.'

Aidan didn't answer. He just swallowed, forcing down the terror.

'But I have to say, Hughes, you've surprised me big time. I never thought you'd have the balls to do something like this. I thought it was the girl who had the cojones, that's why I sent The Mule to her.' He saw Smith look down at the gun still held in Aidan's hand. 'With that too, thought you'd bury it. Whatever, there'll be no shooting here, my kids are around. Mule, come here!' Josef did as he was told. 'Tell Mr Hughes he can't shoot me.'

Josef stepped up to Aidan, briefly he had Smith and his shotgun on one side and The Mule on the other; he was sandwiched between two lethal weapons. Then he felt Josef's breath on his ear.

* * *

May 14th 1997 2.36pm

Blankness.

His mind was totally blank. Where was he? What was he doing? There was a strange smell, of an animal. What was it? Horse, yes, the smell of horse dung.

He was in the stable yard.

He blinked, and found that both Smith and Josef had stepped a little way away from him. It was like he'd slept and woken from a dream. All he knew was that the gun he still held in his right hand was useless and that nothing he could do would let him even point it in the general direction of Smith.

Smith smiled at him. He made a play of putting his own gun down, leaning it against the stable door.

'How does that feel then?' he said. 'Your first little taste of The Mule's power. I can only imagine what it's like, I'll never know. I got that useless Kraut to put a failsafe in The Mule, to condition him so he can never use his power against me.' Smith grinned. 'Just in case the thought crossed your mind.'

At the moment very little was crossing Aidan's mind. It was like he was viewing the world through a fog. It was a struggle to think at all let alone come up with anything cohesive and meaningful.

Oddly, though, this realisation helped; he managed to think of Richard, and Finch, Sam too. This is what it must have been like for them in their last moments. Helpless, confused, their minds invaded, their free will taken away. There was something about that.

He had to fix on it.

'Enjoy the feeling, Hughes,' said Smith. 'Whilst I think what to do with you. What I'll get The Mule to get you to do to yourself. Don't worry, it will be something nice and painful.'

Painful.

He'd lost the thread of his thoughts. The mist returned. Think, find the thread.

Free will.

Free will.

Freedom.

A man who'd had none. Never in his life.

'Josef,' said Aidan. 'I can set you free.'

Both Joseph and Mickey Smith stared at him.

'Josef, what you asked me before. I'll do it.'

'Shut it, Hughes,' said Smith. 'What sort of fucking imbecile are you? I told you, he can't hurt me.'

Aidan raised the gun, not at Smith - which, of course, he couldn't - but at Josef.

'No more box, Josef, no more pain. Freedom.'

Smith said something but Aidan wasn't listening, he'd locked eyes with Josef, with those bland, blank, pale eyes. Suddenly there was something in them, a spark - what was it; realisation? Hope?

Then both Smith and The Mule rushed towards him.

Josef got there first.

* * *

May 14th 1997 2.40pm

Blankness.

His mind was totally blank. Where was he? What was he doing? There was a strange smell, of an animal. What was it? Horse, yes, the smell of horse dung.

He was in the stable yard.

He blinked. The gun was in his hand, smoking.

The Mule - Josef - was at his feet and his man's brains, skull and hair covered Mickey Smith who stood open-mouthed staring down at the man's body.

There was a scream. A young girl's scream. A girl, perhaps thirteen or fourteen, blonde, in jodhpurs and riding boots, a riding helmet on her head.

Somehow the fog was easier to deal with this time. Perhaps The Mule hadn't imposed his thoughts so deeply. Whatever, this time, Aidan was able to act.

He turned round and pointed his gun at the girl.

'I can't shoot you, Smith,' he said. 'But I can shoot your family.'

'Don't you fucking dare,' said Smith. 'You haven't got the balls.'

'Haven't I? Can you risk it, Smith? Can you really?'

He saw Smith's mental struggle. Aidan knew exactly what this meant, this was the man's weak point, the thing he'd used countless times against others, the thing that The Mule had allowed him to take to the extreme.

And, although the girl's terror was something obscene, although Aidan was doing something that was totally alien to him, abhorrent, the same feeling he had when he had threatened the couple on the derelict site came back to him; he had power, it felt good.

Too good.

'Give me your keys,' he said to Smith. 'I'm taking the Range Rover. And her.'

'You're a dead man, Hughes,' said Smith. 'You'll not see another dawn.'

'We'll see about that. Give me the keys.'

Smith tossed them over. Aidan, still with the gun on the girl, grabbed the shotgun too.

'Come on,' he said to the girl. 'We're going for a ride.'

'Daddy!'

'Do as he says, Sophie sweetheart.'

'I'll let her go at the gate,' said Aidan. 'Once I'm out of it of course.'

'You won't get far, Hughes,' growled Smith. 'I'll come for you, and your family.'

'You can come for me,' said Aidan. 'You're welcome to - if you can find me, of course, I intend to make it hard. But if you come for my family, or my friends, or Suzie, I'll come for yours. I got in once, I can do it again. Maybe not to here, but to a school, or somewhere where your wife rides. You can't keep them safe everywhere, every day, Smith.' He looked down at the body. 'You gave me this weapon but I took yours away. You haven't got The Mule anymore to bend people to your will. Goodbye, Smith. See you in hell.'

And goodbye and thank you, Josef, he said to himself as he ushered the girl to the Range Rover.

Chapter Forty-Three

September 2nd 1997, 4.45pm

The low cloud hugged the valley and poured out onto the sea loch like a tenuous ghost of the glaciers that had once been here and carved the land into its present form. There were days when sky was a vivid blue, where the sea sparkled and the little fishing village with its white painted walls seemed to sit on the edge of infinity. Yet the weather always seemed to default to this, where the clouds came down to the water and the world closed in so there was just the village, alone and isolated.

That seemed so appropriate to Aidan.

Not that he was Aidan any more. He was Tom, Thomas Doyle. That was what it said on his Eire passport and driving licence. It was the name that the lads at the building firm where he did labouring work knew him by, though they did call him 'English' as a nickname. It was also the name he'd used to take out this lease on the cottage he shared with Roisin.

He sighed.

Roisin.

He owed her; owed her big time. She had given up her job, sold her flat in Manchester, used her savings and her contacts to get him his false papers, helped him get to Ulster and then over the border to the Republic without leaving a trail, then joined him a few weeks later. She never mentioned it, never reminded him of what he owed her, they hardly touched on the reasons why she'd had to do it. She didn't need to; they both knew why perfectly well.

Which made it worse.

He opened the door and went out into the little garden with its low walls and views of the sea. He could see the yachts moored in the loch, all aligned by the flow of the tide in and out of the basin. He could hear the dank clank of the sheets against the hollow aluminium of the masts, beating out the drum beat that was the soundtrack to his new life. Like him, the yachts rarely ventured far and, when they did, also like him, they always came back.

Oddly, he liked it. He was almost happy.

Almost.

His thoughts drifted back to the same person. They always did, three, four times a day, maybe more, his face haunting Aidan's - Tom's - dreams. The face of another man, trapped in his own life, trapped by his life for what he was and not what he'd done, though he had been used to do plenty. The man who had never known freedom but who had taken that one chance to be free, using Aidan to end it all, to be the executioner. Suicide by failed reporter; that was a new one.

But it was like the baton of imprisonment had been passed from one to another at the point their minds had met.

He looked at his watch. Roisin would be home soon from her job. Maybe she'd have news of home; sometimes she looked for him. Maybe she'd have the paper she sometimes had sent over from Manchester. Suzie had started writing for it again, though, oddly she'd taken on the business correspondent's role. Aidan's job; no, Richard's really. She'd written nothing about Aidan, nothing on Mickey Smith. He wondered why.

He'd like to ask her, but couldn't. That part of his life was over.

He checked his watch again. She'd be back very soon. He'd have to get the kettle on.

He took one last look at the sea. The yachts had swung round slightly, the flow had changed but, essentially, they were still going nowhere.

He nodded to himself and went inside.

NORTHODOX PRESS

HOME OF NORTHERN VOICES

 FACEBOOK.COM/NORTHODOXPRESS

 TWITER.COM/NORTHODOXPRESS

 INSTAGRAM.COM/NORTHODOXPRESS

 NORTHODOX.CO.UK

SUBMISSIONS
ARE OPEN!
WRITER &
DEBUT AUTHOR [ ]
NOVELS &
SHORT FICTION [ ]
FROM OR LIVING
IN THE NORTH [ ]

A NORTHERN STEAMPUNK ADVENTURE

CLOCKWORK
MAGPIES

EMMA WHITEHALL

Printed in Great Britain
by Amazon

10542048R00171